Throw the Dice

An April May Snow

Southern Paranormal Fiction Thriller

By

M. Scott Swanson

[signature: M. Scott Sw...]

April May Snow Titles

Foolish Aspirations
Foolish Beliefs
Foolish Cravings
Foolish Desires
Foolish Expectations
Foolish Fantasies
Foolish Games

Seven Title Prequel Series

Throw the Bouquet

Throw the Cap

Throw the Dice

Throw the Elbow

Throw the Fastball

Throw the Gauntlet

Throw the Hissy

Never miss an April May Snow release.

Join the reader's club!

www.mscottswanson.com

Author's note - This is a work of fiction. Character names, businesses, locations, crime incidents and hauntings are purely imagination. Where the public names of locations are used, please know it is from a place of love and respect from this author. Any resemblance to actual people living or dead or to private events or establishments is entirely coincidental.

A true friend is someone who thinks that you are a good egg even though he knows that you are slightly cracked.
-Bernard Meltzer

Chapter 1

This is not part of my master plan. To say the news puts a crimp in my lifestyle is an understatement.

My recruiter from Master, Lloyd, and Johnson, Jan Miller, continues to drone on about orientation sessions I must complete at the firm. Training sessions that are not scheduled to start for another five weeks.

The training sessions, I expected. The delay in employment is my source of agitation.

Her unexpected news means I am broke this summer.

I struggle to hold my tongue before saying anything that puts a quick, premature end to my career at the prestigious law office in Atlanta. I count the money I have available to live on while Jan talks.

My online account shows five dollars and ten cents available. I add that to the contents of my billfold and change bowl, reaching the staggeringly obscene tally of fifty-two dollars and a penny. On closer inspection, it is a Canadian penny.

I have an issue.

"Are you positive I can't start and do some paralegal work for you until Ramsey can join us for training?" I'm not about to accept this without attempting to find a fair solution for both of us.

"No." Jan gasps. "We believe associates beginning the program together is critical to their development. Synchronization fosters camaraderie and cohesiveness of the team."

I don't understand how my doing paralegal work for five weeks before Ramsey arrives damages our long-term professional relationship. More importantly, Jan never mentioned I would not be starting work with the firm immediately after I graduate from law school.

My diploma—freshly framed with an attractive crimson mat border—lays on my bed. I picked it up this morning from the frame store.

Five minutes ago, I unwrapped the brown protective paper and was flooded with pride as I admired the framed document. April May Snow, Juris Doctorate, University of Alabama.

Having my degree is still surreal. I can hardly believe I managed to hold my plan together all these years and finally accomplish my goal. I get a warm glow over my body as I admire my diploma.

Jan's call jammed a sinister needle into my bubble of happiness.

"Jan, you never mentioned there would be a waiting period before I could start," I remind her.

"Technically, I never told you when you would start. I only said you were awarded one of the two positions." Jan's tone has become terse.

I am smart enough to know I should end the conversation and deal with my new reality. But I don't possess the self-discipline to shut my mouth. "Excuse me if I consider it normal for recruits to expect to start work right after their graduation."

Jan exhales loudly. "I want to remind you that you have not passed the bar yet. You are not an attorney. Master, Lloyd, and Johnson is taking a huge monetary risk investing in your preparation for the bar to help you with your career. There are hundreds of applicants we turned down. We felt you best fit our company's culture. But if this is an inconvenience too monumental for you to overcome—perhaps we were wrong with our decision-making. Perhaps it best we part ways now, April."

It tweaks me that Jan chose to go all nuclear on me. Still, her comment does shift my attitude back into the correct perspective. They are the premier law firm in Atlanta. Their clients are entertainers, sports figures, and successful entrepreneurs. I fought hard for the position and am thrilled to be one of the two selected candidates.

The issue is not the job or my starting date. Being temporarily destitute is the issue.

"No, ma'am. I'm disappointed I'll need to wait to start my career with my new team. I'm anxious to come to work and prove my value."

"I'm pleased to hear you say that," Jan replies. "Understand, you should not be in a rush. You have forty years to work at the firm. Take the next few weeks off, hang out with your friends, and enjoy yourself. You worked hard to finish your degree. Take a few weeks to be young and enjoy not having any responsibilities. You will find it difficult to scratch out any downtime once you start your position with us."

Jan makes an excellent point. The last three years were a grind. Finishing at the top of my class took every ounce of energy I could muster. But with no money and my friends already gone to start their lives, the next five weeks look like purgatory to me.

I finish my conversation with Jan on a positive note. I'm proud to hang up the phone without permanently damaging my career. Staring at the wall, the silence engulfs me, and my ears ring from the silence.

The thing is, I would love nothing more than to kick back and take an extended vacation. I earned a break.

The problem being I failed to plan for a five-week vacation after school, and I didn't save any money for summer expenses. If I had known there would be a delay after graduation before I could start work, I would have—Oh, who am I kidding? I have been operating broke for so long that no money in my wallet is my norm. If Jan had warned me, I would be in the exact same financial crunch.

My parents hold a hard-and-fast rule concerning college. They pay for undergraduate degrees for their children.

One of my twin brothers and I took advantage of their promise. My other twin brother went to work in the family business after high school.

According to the family rule, graduate degrees are not my parents' responsibility. I was on my own for graduate school. Here is a fun fact for you, law school isn't cheap.

I'm not complaining. What a wonderful gift that my parents paid for my undergraduate degree. They even bent their rule and continued to pay my rent and utilities as if those bills did not constitute "school expenses" while I worked on my law degree.

Still, the student loans I took out for the three years of law school would buy me a comfortable brick house in my hometown of Guntersville, Alabama.

Not that I would ever buy a house in Guntersville. It is the last place I would want to own a home. One of the specific reasons I went to law school is to make sure I do not end up in my hometown.

I'm considering my options—slim and none—when I remember the lease on my apartment ends this Wednesday. Great. Now I also must figure out what I'm going to do with my stuff. This keeps getting better.

Focus, April. This is no time to think negatively.

I can be sure I will not survive on fifty-two dollars over five weeks. I can be frugal, but even ramen noodles run more than ten dollars a week.

I suppose I could crash at the sorority house for a few weeks in a pinch. With most of the girls gone for the summer break, I'm sure my sorority can find room for me. I could help them prepare for this fall's rush while I'm there.

Honestly, I'm not exactly enthused about the idea. But my best friend Marty left for DC yesterday, and the sorority house might be my only bet.

I pick up the phone and call the president, Breanna Coggins. Breanna sort of owes me a favor since I helped decorate the house for graduation last week.

"April?"

I'm saved on her phone. That must be a good sign. Right? "Hi, Breanna. How is your summer going?"

"Busy." She hiccups an abbreviated laugh. "Are you calling me from Atlanta?"

My ears warm as extra blood rushes to them. I have no idea why I should be embarrassed. "Oh, no. My job doesn't start for a few weeks."

"Oh," she says. "I thought you were leaving right after graduation."

"I was—at least it was my intention. But I thought about my circumstances the next morning, realizing I'm only twenty-seven. I have forty years to work at the firm. I've worked hard. So, I might as well take some time before I start." Just because the words came from Jan Miller's mouth does not make the advice any less true.

"That makes sense. Well, if you're bored, come on by for dinner. I'm sure the girls would love to visit with you," Breanna offers.

"Funny you should mention visiting. You see, I already turned in my notice to my landlord, and I've lost the lease on my apartment. I was wondering if you might find a room I could use for a few weeks and a place for me to store my stuff?"

The long pause catches me off guard. I pull the phone from my ear to check that I have not accidentally disconnected Breanna.

"Wow, April. I hate to hear about your apartment lease. The girls and I would love to help, but we doubled up in the rooms the past year. Even though a lot of the girls left for the summer, all the rooms are occupied right now."

My buoyant spirits flag. "I don't mind sharing a room."

"Yeah, I don't know. I wouldn't feel right about asking the girls. They pay a steep price for the rooms. The ones staying behind consider the solo room a bonus where they get a room to themselves for a couple of months."

My chest tightens, and I have difficulty breathing. "I won't be any trouble to a roommate. I won't even be at the house most of the time. There is so much to do getting ready for my move to Atlanta."

Breanna blows into the receiver again. Boy, that is becoming annoying. "I suppose we could give you the sofa in the den. I've been told it's comfortable."

I am in shock. After all the hours I spent on behalf of my

sorority, and this is how they pay me back?

Breanna is not done cutting me down to size. "We definitely don't have room for furnishings, though. You'll need to rent a storage unit."

I am so numb I barely squeak out, "Sure."

"Okay." Breanna's syrupy voice returns. "I'll tell the girls you'll be staying with us. They'll enjoy your little summer visit."

I try to tell myself this is not personal. The sorority grew exponentially in popularity in the seven years I was on campus.

But gosh darn it, a good bit of why the sorority has become so popular is because of the leadership I provided. Because I did a fantastic job as the president, I earned a five-week stay on a ratty sofa rather than the spare room I deserve.

Whatever. Beggars can't be choosers.

Chapter 2

I search for storage units on my phone and call one with the cute name of Packrat.

The pleasant-sounding lady asks me several questions. We determine I'll need a twelve-foot by twenty-foot unit. The size sounds reasonable if I stack my belongings.

The $160 a month cost with a $150 deposit does not sound reasonable. I choke as I regain my composure and tell her I must discuss the cost with my roommate.

To recount, for the privilege of sleeping on a crummy sofa, I will need to ante up $310. Oh, I forgot the U-Haul rental. I mustn't forget the moving trailer, assuming I can rig my Prius with a trailer hitch. Hopefully, the exertion will not cause my ten-year-old car to blow a piston.

Peaches! I'm easily looking at four hundred dollars. That's if I don't kill my car during the move.

The financial expense is before I deal with the social implications of me—a newly minted lawyer and former leader of the sorority—being relegated to sleeping on the girls' party sofa. Most of my sorority sisters look up to me as someone they hope to emulate. There is no telling how many fragile psyches I will damage by temporarily being homeless and camped out on their sofa.

I think I knew from the start. The sorority house option is a hard no.

This is not the time for wishful thinking. Still, I can't resist gravitating toward Granny Snow's belief she can manifest anything by asking the universe and focusing her energies on the item. She calls the process manifestation.

How cool would it be if I could make ten thousand dollars appear right now? Heck, why limit myself? I would wish for a hundred thousand dollars and give twenty thousand to charity.

Still, that power over the universe does not exist. It is simply Granny's entertaining, whimsical nonsense. Never one to allow a joke to be one-dimensional, she insists I also have the ability. To date, the only thing I have ever manifested is aggravating circumstances.

The way I understand my situation, I have three options available to me. Two are disagreeable, and one is improbable.

I can call Daddy this second, and he will wire me any amount of money I ask him to send. As long as I swear to never tell Mama he helped me with cash. Of course, we will call it a loan. Still, the "First Father Bank of Alabama" charges their favorite customer a zero-percent interest rate, and repayment dates are dubious at best.

Considering I want to be taken seriously as an adult, I do not want to call Daddy for help. Asking for assistance so soon after the graduation party my parents threw for me seems like backsliding.

I can always show up at my parents' lake house. Last week, Mama complained because I was heading straight to Atlanta rather than visiting the family in Guntersville first. I'm not sure if five weeks is technically a visit or the first stages of building toward squatter rights.

The biggest problem with the surprise visit to Guntersville plan is Mama and my brother Dusty. After a week or two, those two will grow suspicious and start asking uncomfortable questions about my employment status. They are sharp like that. Given I am officially the world's worst liar, I best not put myself in a situation where I will feel the need to construct some long-winded story to explain why I haven't left for Atlanta yet.

The third choice is a real long shot. But given the fact the first two options bite so bad, I need to investigate the third before I rule any options out.

My hope is I can strike a deal with my apartment manager. Perhaps I can scrape enough money together by pawning my personal items. I can always buy back any I want when I receive my relocation check from the law firm.

I call the rental office as I pace through my apartment, searching for anything of value to pawn. The phone rings ten times before going to voicemail.

I hang up, wait ten seconds, and call the office again.

I have numerous formal dresses I could sell, but the season is a few months off. I own a new elliptical machine, a graduation gift I will be exercising with once I am settled in Atlanta. The only other item I own of value is a hand-me-down TV I remember watching Barney on as a kid.

Mary, the live-in leasing agent, better be in a charitable mood. If not, I'm back to calling Daddy for that loan. The leasing office phone goes to voicemail again.

Perfect. The one time I need somebody in the office, and everyone has gone to lunch.

I cannot leave a voicemail and hope for a callback. I need an answer today, so I can develop a plan. I slide my phone into my back pocket and head out for the office.

The wet, blanketing heat sucks my breath away. I have lived in Alabama my entire life, and I still am amazed how the air can be too hot to breathe. As I make my way across the freshly tarred asphalt parking lot, little rivulets of sweat trace down my back. It is so blasted hot today there isn't a single soul at the swimming pool. Everyone is inside, huddled close to their air conditioning vents.

What the heck? Mary's car is out front, so she must be inside. I yank the office door open and suck the cooler air deep into my lungs.

"April?"

I open my eyes, wiping my damp eyebrows with the back of my wrist. The tiny woman in front of me looks vaguely familiar. Still, I can't place her face. "Yes?"

She taps her chest. "April, it's me, Sonia Jurgensen."

Man, I must be a hundred years old. The last time I saw Sonia Jurgensen, she was doing an age-inappropriate dance with her cheerleading squad. "Oh, my goodness. I didn't recognize you. It's been so long."

She grins in the wild-eyed manner she always has. "I know. Like what—ten years?"

"Goodness, where's the time gone?" We stare at one another before I add. "When did you start at Alabama?"

Sonia jerks her chin into the air and lets out a manic laugh, making the hair on the back of my neck stand up. "Oh, I'm not in college, silly." She turns and pulls a young man forward. "Trent here is the college boy. We're going steady, and I'm moving in with him."

I struggle to close my mouth. Sonia is ecstatic, but I do not understand why. "Well, that's awfully cool."

Her lips flatten as she takes a serious tone. "I know. Right? Not everybody can find their true love before they're twenty."

I nod my head slowly. "True. Few people are that fortunate."

"Of course, both of our parents are totally against the marriage." She gestures randomly with her hand. "The whole 'you're too young, why don't you date other people'—But I say if you found 'the one,' what's the point? You don't want to lose them. That's for sure."

This is becoming more awkward by the minute. "I'm sure they have your best interest at heart."

She rolls her eyes. "The last straw was when my mom asked if I was pregnant. Like we have to be pregnant to want to spend the rest of our lives together! I just don't feel the need to explain to them anymore why we're in love, and to constantly justify it to them."

Sonia's crazy eyes make gooseflesh prickle up across my shoulder, and I force another smile. Seeking refuge from her mania, I direct my next question to her boyfriend. "Trent, what are you studying?"

"Quantitative analysis with a minor in statistics." His eyes are as crazy as hers.

I shudder involuntarily. Trent and Sonia are two peas in a pod. Two crazy peas. "Well, that's a curriculum that'll keep you busy."

He goes wide-eyed and grins. "I can do standard deviation calculations in my head."

And I can pick out a deviant. "Impressive."

Mary enters from the back room and pulls up short as she notices me. "Hey, April."

"Hi, Mary."

"Give me a moment to finish up with Trent and Sonia." She hands Sonia a key. "I need you to sign here."

As Sonia leans over and signs her name, she asks, "Do you have any lunch plans, April?"

I stammer since Sonia caught me unprepared. "Uh—well, no. I need to put my things in order before I leave for Atlanta. I start my new job in a few weeks."

"Oh, that sounds fun. I've always wanted to travel the world." She turns to Trent. "Weren't we just saying the other day we would love to visit Georgia?"

"Sure did, babe."

Sonia runs a hand down my arm. "You have to come to lunch with us and tell us all about your job."

"There's not much to tell." That is an understatement. I have never been to Atlanta myself. A fact becoming more preposterous to me the closer I come to moving day.

"Sure, there is." She plants her hands on her hips. "I won't take no for an answer, April."

Trent shrugs. "That's a fact. She never takes no for an answer."

"What can I do for you, April?" Mary interjects thankfully into the craziness.

"Uh, I—" I raise my eyebrows at Sonia and Trent in hopes they will take the hint and give us some privacy.

"No worries. We're all family here," Sonia says.

"Do you have a leak or something, April?" Mary continues to press.

"No." I scan from Mary to Sonia and back as I blow out an exasperated breath. Whatever. I grew up in a town where everyone was into each other's business. I do not understand why sharing would bother me now.

"I was notified I won't be starting in Atlanta for a few days. I'm wondering if you leased out my apartment yet?" I ask.

Mary's brow furrows. "A few days? Like a week?"

"Hmm—more like five," I say under my breath.

"Five days…"

"Weeks."

"Oh." Mary sucks in a breath. "Almost the entire summer."

"You've already rented my apartment?" Lord, I am going to have to call Daddy. How embarrassing.

"No. I'm scheduled to show your place to a new student on Friday. But I haven't issued a contract yet."

My shoulders relax, and I can breathe again. "What a relief."

I remember my parents telling me once they only paid half-rate during the summers. Maybe I can negotiate an even lower rental rate. "Do you have an economy summer rate? My roommate has already left, and I'll be footing the entire bill."

"We drop the rent to half price during the summer, but if your roommate has already left—"

I catch her drift. "That *is* my normal rate."

Mary wrinkles her nose. "I suppose this isn't what you hoped to hear. I'm sorry."

"It's not your fault." I freeze up as I do the rent calculations in my head. "Nine hundred dollars per month?"

"I'm afraid so."

Whatever. I will have to sign the deal and figure the cash part out later. One thing is for sure, I can't wait and risk losing the apartment to someone else. I really would be on the street then. "I'll take it."

"Alright." Mary opens a drawer and produces a blue sheet of paper. "I'll need you to sign this summer contract, and we're all set."

All set except for how I plan to come up with the money. "Excellent." I lean over Mary's desk and lift the pen to sign the document.

My natural desire to understand everything around me and the multiple contract law courses I completed hijack my sensibilities. I begin to read the contract rather than sign it.

"When I was eight, my mom and I got kicked out of our rental. The landlord put everything we owned out in front of the trailer."

Sonia's voice is breaking my concentration. A clause in the contract does not make sense to me.

"I had gotten one of those Betty Crocker bake ovens for Christmas from my grandmother. You remember those. Don't you, April?"

I hold up a finger to Sonia as I re-read the disconcerting clause on the contract. "Mary, what does this mean? Payment in full? And three months?"

"Just a summer contract thing, April. Since it is half-rate and usually the renters have gone home, we collect all three months' rent upfront."

"The oven was gone when I got home. They left all the ratty Beanie Babies my mom collected, but someone stole my Betty Crocker bake oven." Sonia finishes her story.

"But I only need two months," I say.

"I wish I was around for you, baby." At least Trent is listening to Sonia's sob story. "It makes me so sad and angry every time you tell that story. I want to throat punch whoever did my girl dirty."

"You're such a sweetie," Sonia says. A wet smacking noise starts up behind me.

"Two months would be the standard rate. You are better off with the three months at half price."

Mary is correct. Still, the deal feels like I am paying for much more than I want. I never considered who owned the apartment complex. With rules and discounts like these, I would expect them to be relatives of Tony Soprano. "I need to think about it."

Mary purses her lips. "I've already written the contract using your deposit for the third month since you are leaving. That lowers your payment from twenty-seven hundred dollars to eighteen hundred."

I can barely conceal my temper. I will not be getting back my share of the deposit—my parents' deposit—which I had counted on until the relocation check comes in from my firm. Essentially, I will pay the apartment complex for a month when I will already be in Atlanta. I slide the sheet back to Mary. "I think I'm going to check out my other options."

With a click of her tongue, Mary pulls the sheet back. "It's probably for the best. The guy wanting to lease your apartment is an incoming freshman. Renting the unit to him this summer will work out better for the apartment complex. He might be here another four or five years."

I pull the sheet back from Mary and sign on the line. "On second thought, you're right. Half-priced rent makes rent almost painless."

There is a louder smacking noise behind me. I turn to find Trent and Sonia lip-locked. They are kissing with such fervor it resembles an above-the-neck wrestling match more than a kiss.

I wave to Mary as I step toward the door. "Thank you for your help, Mary."

She squinches up her face. "Hey. Aren't you forgetting something?"

My keys are in my pocket, and I'm leaving the lovebirds with Mary. No, I'm all set. "What's that?"

"The payment. I need eighteen hundred dollars now. The contract has to be paid in full."

My breath rushes out of me. "Eighteen hundred dollars?" I parrot.

"Summer rules." Mary acts like her explanation makes the amount more palatable.

I pull at my ponytail. "I left my checkbook in my apartment."

Trent stops assaulting Sonia with his gaping mouth and shoots me a crooked smile. "You have a checkbook? I didn't think they still made those."

"Sure, they do," I snipe back. I haven't ever had one, but I'm sure banks will still send you checkbooks if you ask for them.

"We don't take personal checks anymore, April," Mary continues with a frown. "But if you can bring me a cashier's check by Wednesday, that will work."

I try to act nonchalant, but I cross my chest with my arms as I begin to fidget. "Perfect. I'll bring you a check Wednesday morning."

With the briefest offer of a smile toward Mary, I open the door. I can't leave the situation behind me quickly enough.

Chapter 3

Moments like this are when I realize what a brat I have been my entire life. For too long, Mama and Daddy simply took care of any issues causing me trouble or anxiety. I'm a new person now, and those days are officially over. I'm the new-and-improved, accountable-to-the-world April May Snow.

Being accountable sucks.

Putting on the mantle of responsibility also feels awkward. Probably because when I try to act responsibly … mostly I feel like an imposter.

"April, hold up!" Sonia is close on my heels, with Trent jogging behind her.

"Can we talk?" she asks.

I gesture over my shoulder toward my apartment. "I don't think so, Sonia. I'm sort of busy."

She cocks her head to the left. The lower half of her face is flushed red from the aggressive kiss she shared with Trent. "I couldn't help but overhear you have some money issues."

Exactly why I didn't want them in the room when I was talking to Mary. "I don't have any money issues," I respond as I pull up to full height.

"If you write a check for eighteen hundred dollars, is the check going to clear or bounce?" Trent asks as he pulls up level with Sonia.

My eyes roll involuntarily. "What's it to you anyway?"

Trent shrugs. "It doesn't mean much of anything to me. Except we might be able to help each other."

All the gong-like danger alarms in my head clang loudly. Gooseflesh breaks out across my body. "I doubt it."

Trent laughs. "No. I have a money-making idea. Sonia and I were planning on trying out my hypothesis this week, but her car went on the blitz. You have a car. Right?"

I stare at him with a droll expression.

"True story, April." Sonia steps between us to break our stare-off. "They say the alternator is dead, and the fuel pump needs replacing."

With that many things wrong, Sonia either needs an honest mechanic or a new car. "What does my car have to do with your big idea?"

Trent steps to the side and back into view as he favors me with a sly smile. "Transportation, of course."

Trent and I continue to stare at one another. The boy obviously believes he has explained everything. I still have no clue what is going on.

Sonia puts her hand on Trent's forearm. "Sweetie, you need to fill April in on the details." Sonia directs her attention to me. "Trent has developed a surefire way to track card play during a game. We plan to drive down to the casino in Montgomery and win enough money for an engagement ring. Then we can do things up right once we win the money."

There is a lot to unpack in Sonia's statement. I try to keep the condescension out of my voice, but I do less than an admirable job. "You do realize the Windsong Casino in Montgomery does *not* have any tables."

Trent's eyebrows become one. "For real?"

"Yep. Strictly slots."

"Well, what sort of casino doesn't run tables?" Trent asks.

"I suppose one not wanting to pay for much labor. You would have to go to Biloxi to play cards."

"Mississippi?" Sonia asks.

I'm reasonably sure no other state has a Biloxi. "Yes." Another stream of sweat rolls down my back. I'm losing patience with this conversation.

"You always said you wanted to see the ocean, baby." Trent places his hand casually on Sonia's hips as he pulls her to his side.

"Is that true, April? Is Biloxi near the ocean?"

I shrug. "Well, it's the gulf. But it is saltwater."

"How far is it?" she asks.

I take my time calculating in my head. "I guess about four hours."

Sonia gasps. "Four hours?" She bounces on the balls of her feet. "Do you hear her, Trent? Just a four-hour drive. Then we can check off our first state visit *and* see a real ocean."

Trent gives her a hug. "Such exciting stuff, baby." He turns his attention to me. "If I pay for the gas, eats, and the room, you'll drive us?"

We must have skipped a step in our conversation. "Uh—no."

Trent's face flushes red as the muscles in his jaw flex. I take note his temper is sort of sudden. "Why not?" he asks.

"Well, for starters, those casinos are trained to spot folks who are counting cards."

"I'm not counting cards. I'm working the statistical probability of the next card played."

I can't stop a bark of laughter from escaping me. I know it's not wise to laugh at hotheaded, wild-eyed Southern boys, but the laugh slips out. "News flash, Trent. They call your statistical probability formula 'counting cards.'"

"His method is foolproof, April. He played last week at Billy Johnson's poker game and won huge," Sonia explains.

"I don't think Billy Johnson is trained in identifying card counters." I shake my head in disbelief and start walking to my apartment.

"Man, for a chick who is all educated, you're not real bright."

The words are a hot poker on my backside. I spin on my heels and track back toward Trent. "What did you say?"

"You heard me just fine. There's nothing wrong with your

hearing."

My temper slips a gear. I'm struggling to keep my crazy on a leash. "I'll tell you what's not smart, is going to a casino and thinking you're going to pull something over on them. Those folks have been identifying scammers for years. Your little scheme doesn't stand a chance against professionals. Besides, they make a habit of throwing cheats under the jail. *If* they take them to jail. If you play your stupid gambit on them, you're just as liable to end up as gator poop by next weekend."

"Well, I guess we're not gonna find out now, are we?" Trent snipes.

"I guess not." I give him the nastiest stink eye I can work up.

"I suppose I had you all wrong," Trent continues. "I thought a road trip to the casino would be a kick in the pants for the three of us. Especially when we win a hundred thousand dollars."

Vertigo washes over me so forcefully that I stagger two steps to my left and reach out to catch myself against a parked car. This is not happening. It's totally a coincidence Trent mentioned a hundred thousand dollars.

"Forget it. You're probably one of those chicks who couldn't enjoy winning a fortune. You'd probably have to do something stupid like give twenty thousand of your winnings to a charity or something."

So much for coincidences. Trent verbalized precisely what I wished for less than an hour earlier. I can't go there. The last thing I need right now is to give life to Granny's quirky manifestation ideas.

The mental partition I worked so diligently to create in my mind has crumbled in the last few weeks. No matter how I push against my psychic abilities, including telepathy and the ability to perceive the paranormal, they grow stronger. If I add manifestation to the "April the freak" list, I might end up at Bryce Mental Hospital by the end of the week.

"Besides, where are you going to come up with the eighteen hundred dollars you need for your apartment?" Trent presses me.

I struggle to balance myself and release my hold on the car. "And this is your business, how?"

Sonia clutches Trent's forearm again. "Come on, sweetie. If she doesn't want to go, we can't force her."

"Hold on a moment, baby." Trent rubs his forehead with the palm of his hand. "I don't understand. But I have this premonition that April is supposed to go on this trip. I can't put my finger on a specific reason. But I believe it will be a huge mistake if we don't convince her."

With fifty-two dollars to my name, I need a minimum of eighteen hundred by Wednesday. I have nothing worth pawning, and the most significant asset I own is my worn-out Prius. Honestly, what do I have to lose? "I'll take you."

"You will?" Sonia asks.

Trent appears relieved as he exhales. "Cool. Sonia and I will go home and pack." He sets his face with a stern expression as he nods his head. "I appreciate you doing this."

Sonia jumps up and down. "We're going, baby. I'm so excited."

As I watch the two lovebirds walk toward the other side of the apartment complex, I wonder what I have gotten myself into. But as much as I want to be disgusted with my decision, what other play do I have? Call Daddy and ask for a loan? Crash on the sorority's couch for the next five weeks? No. I am taking the one shot available to me. I hope my fifty-two dollars can hold out long enough for the manifestation powers to do their thing.

I shake my head and walk toward my apartment to pack a bag. Wouldn't it be a hoot to win a hundred thousand dollars? Hey, you need to have dreams.

Chapter 4

Within the hour, we load the Prius and head down Interstate 20. Sonia insists on sitting in Trent's lap in the front seat of the Prius. I want to object. I mean, I don't care to have the police write me a ticket because they are not properly buckled up.

Still, in a few hours, the casino manager will be reporting us to the police. We will be in a whole heap of trouble with the law then, so why worry about a traffic ticket.

I'm not a chicken. I am, however, a rule follower most of the time. I will need to clarify that they are on their own with their card counting. I do not want to be involved with that scheme. I will have to figure out how to make my few dollars grow into at least eighteen hundred on my own.

As we come into Eutaw, Trent speaks up. "How's your gas?"

I'm under a quarter of a tank. "We probably need to fill up."

"There's a plan. I need to empty my tank." He shifts Sonia out of his lap onto his thighs. "You're about to squeeze it out of me, baby."

"I'm sorry," Sonia says before kissing Trent's cheek.

"Y'all want a bucket of chicken?" Trent asks.

"Sounds yummy," Sonia says.

Driving and eating fried chicken. Two things that do not go together. But I suppose I'm not in the position to turn down a free meal while I'm playing destitute chauffeur. "I'll second the motion."

We pass through Meridian an hour later. The sun is setting, and the chicken is gone. Except for the cloying, heavy oil scent hanging in the car. Trent has impossibly folded onto the backseat and is snoring lightly.

"I realize you're disappointed in me."

Sonia's voice startles me. "Why do you say that?"

Sonia stares out the passenger window. "The expression on your face when I told you I was moving in with Trent."

I bite at concealing my emotions. My lack of expression control is one of the reasons I am the worst liar in the world. "I'm disappointed *for* you, not *in* you. You have a lot of potential. I don't want you to sell yourself short."

"Believe it or not, I'm getting exactly what I want. I want a family. A close family."

I'm not up to speed on Sonia's current situation, but I remember her mother raised her on her own. I don't have anything to add to the conversation. I stare ahead into the inky, dark night.

"With your extended family, you can't understand. But a family of my own is important to me."

"If a family is what you want, who am I to judge, Sonia? If you're working toward what is important to you, that's enough to make it important. I wouldn't stop you from living your life the way you need to and not expect you to judge me in return." I shrug. "Besides, my opinion shouldn't count anyway."

"But your opinion does matter." She shifts closer to me. "It means a lot to me, April."

I don't understand. I haven't seen Sonia in ten years, and now my opinion of her choice in men is significant?

The thing is, this is not an uncommon occurrence for me. I'm glad my time at the sorority finally ended precisely because of this sort of thing. It is a lot of responsibility when people decide your opinion counts for something.

"If you love him and he makes you happy, I guess you have something special, Sonia. Does he treat you well?"

She flashes a beautiful smile, and I can answer my own question before she says, "Like a princess."

"Growing up, isn't the tiara what we all wanted? I guess you're one of the lucky ones."

She settles back into her seat. "I am. Aren't I?"

A few minutes later, Sonia's soft baby snores from the passenger seat are louder than the hum of my car's tires. The dark, thick Mississippi night and a long stretch of lonesome highway are the only company I keep now.

My hand automatically reaches for the radio, and I think better. The noise might wake up my passengers. I'm not in the mood to talk anymore tonight.

I'm having a challenging time getting over the unfairness of my law firm not telling me when they hired me that I would not start immediately. If I had known three months ago, I could have the entire time scheduled with my family and paid for.

What an incredible celebration vacation that could have been for me. I would have appreciated the rest and relaxation. A perfect reset to clear my mind and prepare for the next uphill push in my life. Full partnership at the law firm.

But I became officially on my own when my parents left my graduation last weekend. I'm supposed to be an adult now. I can't bring myself to call them and ask for help when I have only been doing this adulting thing for two days.

Most of all, I don't want to be a loser.

I guess Sonia and I may have more in common than I initially thought. She says my opinion matters to her. I worry about people's opinions of me, too. Still, I believe I may have a better handle on whose opinion counts than Sonia.

My sorority sisters' opinion of me used to hold a lot of weight. I still care enough not to embarrass myself by sleeping on a sofa in their den. I don't want the "loser" moniker. But I think I already realize that what those girls think of me will hardly matter in two years.

My family's opinion, on the other hand, matters a lot.

Sometimes I think of myself as this bundle of angst-ridden mediocrity surrounded by family members known for some exceptional trait. Daddy is brilliant and patient, Mama is creative and beautiful, Dusty turns everything into money, and Chase is the coolest person I've ever met. Me? About the only thing I'm decent at is working a plan.

"How far do we have?"

The voice in my right ear makes me nearly jump out of my skin. "Bless it, Trent. I didn't realize you were up."

"Your thinking is too loud."

I steal a glance at him to my right. His elbows are propped on both front seats and are inches from my ear. "I think about two hours."

He nods his acknowledgment. "This is a whole new level of dark out here."

We ride in companionable silence. I resist the urge to ask Trent to hand me a napkin so I might bump his hand and get a more precise read on his spirit. I'm becoming more confident that he has a shiny core. At least I'm not getting the prickly feeling I get around evil people.

Still, he does have those extra-sharp predatory eyes. In my experience, folks with those eyes are a little unpredictable. I hope Trent is one of the few exceptions.

I would like to say I want to better understand him because I have a personal stake now. I mean, Sonia claims my opinion of Trent is important to her. It would be easier to derive my opinion if I could touch Trent and figure out what makes him tick.

But mostly, I'm just nosy.

The struggle not to use my psychic skill on Trent is real.

But there is my conundrum. I must become disciplined or, better yet, squash my psychic abilities altogether if I'm going to live in a normal society. An involuntary shudder works up my spine as I think of my Nana living in a trailer alone in the woods.

No, I want to be a lawyer. The job is stressful enough without people's thoughts rolling into my head if I touch them. Seeing and hearing ghosts would be even less helpful. Any useful information I might gain from using my "gifts" would be offset by the danger of simply scrambling my brain with too much stimuli.

"Have you been here before?" Trent asks.

THROW THE DICE : APRIL MAY SNOW PSYCHIC MYSTERY #3

"I have a second cousin who lives in Gulfport. My parents used to drive us down each summer to visit for a weekend."

"Sounds cool. My parents do a hog roast every Fourth of July. Since it is our annual reunion, I see all my extended family at the event. I'm looking forward to taking Sonia to it this year."

I say it before I realize, "How long have y'all been dating?"

"Only six weeks."

"Moving sort of quick, aren't y'all?"

"You think?" His tone is full of sarcasm.

"But what do I know?" It's time for me to be quiet.

"No, I get it. If one of my friends were moving this quickly with a girl, I would probably question him." I watch him reach out and move a stray lock of hair from Sonia's face. "But somehow, I know this is right. And I'm not one to risk a sure thing."

I need to stay out of their business. But I can't help myself. "Why risk trouble with this card-counting scheme?"

He laughs as he leans back in the seat. "Don't take me wrong. I could use the cash. But I want to confirm my theory works. If it doesn't, and my calculations are wrong, so be it. I'm simply curious if the statistics hold like I think they will."

Trent sounds like all the men in my family. They are constantly testing and trying new things.

"Do you have a plan?" Trent asks.

"What do you mean?"

"I expect you might have formulated a plan on how to win the money you need and a backup plan in case you don't." Trent draws a breath and exhales dramatically. "Lord knows this road would be perfect for designing plans in your head."

Trent's question helps me realize that I don't have a plan for the first time in twenty years. I'm naked without a plan.

"You didn't ask for any advice, but I'd stay away from the slots if I were you."

"Why?" I ask.

"They're for crap on return. Slots are set up to mostly eat time and slowly drain you of your cash. I would start out with the blackjack tables. Something simple, you can control better."

"Back to the card counting proposition," I say harsher than I intend.

"Nah, you don't need to count cards to win at blackjack. It doesn't hurt, but it's not necessary."

Okay. I now have a plan. Or at least the start of a plan. I'll play blackjack until I win enough money to try and win some fast cash. I pray I am right that this trip is meant to be from some manifestation I pulled off without trying. "Thank you for the pointers."

"No worries." I watch his reflection in the rearview mirror as he stretches. "Do you want me to drive a bit? I'm not a bad driver. I had to sell my motorcycle to cover my tuition last semester."

"I'm good. Like you say, the road is perfect for thinking, and I have some things I need to work out."

"Your choice. I'm going to get some more shuteye. Wake me up if you change your mind."

This must be some form of manifestation I'm creating despite not understanding how or what I'm doing. The impromptu road trip with an old acquaintance and her boyfriend feels too ordinary when it should seem downright odd.

Not to mention an incredibly low probability of occurrence.

The biggest thing convincing me I'm creating these events is the incessant sensation of being pulled in the direction of Biloxi. Something is calling me. It must be the hundred thousand dollars I plan on winning.

Chapter 5

To my surprise, the casinos are still hopping when we arrive a little before two in the morning. I pull in under the awning of the Biloxi Queen and stretch before I turn off the motor.

"All right, sleeping beauties. Let's get up to the room," I say in my best drill sergeant voice.

"I'll bring the bags," Trent offers as he opens his door.

Sonia sits up as her eyes open large. "Oh, Lordy. It's more beautiful than I ever expected. Trent, look. It's like a castle."

"I told you it would be, baby. One castle for my princess." Trent pulls the last of our bags from the hatch.

"And the ocean. I think I hear the ocean," she says.

"I'm not sure I can hear it, but I certainly smell it," Trent says with a wrinkle of his nose as he gathers up the luggage.

I move to take my backpack and travel case. "I've got mine, Trent."

"You sure? It's no trouble."

As I take my luggage from Trent, a middle-aged man dressed in a gold uniform comes out of the hotel with a cart. "Hi, folks. Let me take those for you." He reaches for Trent's luggage.

Trent pulls his duffel bag back. "Hey, we've got this, buddy."

"No, I insist."

It takes me a moment to understand why Trent is resisting help. At first, I think some macho syndrome might be forcing him to do everything himself. But when the valet approaches me and asks for my car keys, the lightbulb goes off in my mind.

"No, thank you. I'll park it myself."

The valet sneers. "Your choice. Enjoy the walk, lady."

I'm not sure if I will enjoy the walk, but I will enjoy keeping the twenty bucks I can bet at the blackjack table. Personalized service is excellent when you can afford it, but I need every dollar I can hold on to for now.

"We'll wait for you at the front desk," Trent tells me as he reaches for my luggage again.

This time I understand and am grateful for his assistance. "Thank you."

The valet was not kidding. The lot is filled all the way to the row adjacent to the frontage road.

I exit my car and click the lock button twice. You never know who might want a ten-year-old Prius with a hundred and fifty thousand miles.

As I walk back toward the casino entrance, I take in the grandness of the building for the first time. The flowing lines of its tastefully lit facade give it the appearance of an enchanted castle. It would fit nicely on the Las Vegas strip, only it is smaller than those mega-casinos.

The cool, salty air lifts my hair, and I smell a slight brackish decay. The scent of decaying vegetation fuses my brain's unrelated synapses. The partition I always keep in my mind develops a gaping hole.

Voices roll into my mind with uncontrolled, excited chatter. Deep bass and high-pitched soprano voices tumble into my mind. Each is discernibly different. Still, speaking on top of one another, I cannot understand any of them.

The onslaught of the dead's conversations gives me a case of vertigo as I reach the front door. I endure the stink eye of the valet and hurry past him as I'm sure soon I will be seeing my fried chicken dinner again. My only hope is the voices might quiet once I enter the hotel.

The voices do lower a notch once I'm inside. I struggle to keep my balance as I make my way to one of several trees inside the brick-and-tile entryway. I lean against one of the trees while I clear my mind so I may reestablish the partition between real-life senses and the supernatural.

This is my recent normal as the powers I thought had left me while I was in college come back with more strength and easier access than ever before in my life. My grandmothers call the freakish paranormal powers my "gifts." I consider them my curse.

Since the age of eight, the day I briefly drowned, I have possessed the ability to see and hear supernatural entities. The ability continued to strengthen until I reached womanhood at twelve. Then it crescendoed overnight. It became so overwhelming I could not function during the day. All day, I heard dispossessed spirits who tried to tell me what happened to them or explain what they needed me to do to help.

My Nana—who half the town thinks is a hippie, and the other half thinks she is a witch, both would be right—instructed me on the art of building blocking partitions in my mind. This trick served me well over the last fifteen years, but events in the previous few weeks have woken the ability. Frankly, I'm afraid I am losing control. It scares the fire out of me.

"April?"

Sonia comes into view. "Hey."

She cocks her head. "Are you alright? You're green around the lips."

"I'm tuckered out. This has been a long day."

"I'll second that." She flashes a grin. "But isn't it worth it? Look at this place. It is an absolute palace."

I would love to join her awestruck happiness. And the entryway is impressive. But I find it difficult to be impressed by architectural achievements when my mouth is watering as if I'm about to throw up. "It's right uptown."

Sonia reaches out and takes me by the elbow. "Let's go to the room. Trent has already headed up with the luggage."

Oddly, as Sonia squeezes my elbow, the last voices leave while the churning in my stomach subsides. I allow her to lead me toward the elevator as I set about the task of resetting the partitions in my mind.

"Can you believe they have trees? Real live trees in here?" Sonia asks as she presses the elevator button. "How do they keep them alive?"

I gaze up and point. "Skylights. They allow natural light in."

"Wow, so cool. You're smart, April."

If I were so intelligent, I would have considered that a casino would be loaded with emotions attached to the building. Not everything I hear in my mind is from dead people. Sometimes the voices come from residual energies left by people's outbursts of anger or happiness.

"You would've figured it out. You're too excited since it's all new to you."

Sonia blushes, turning her attention to her bare feet. "Maybe."

I smile as I try to lighten the mood while we wait in the elevator. "I figured you would've headed straight outdoors as badly as you wanted to see the ocean."

"I wanted to. But Trent says the sun will be up in a few hours, and it will be more beautiful at sunrise."

The elevator arrives, and we step in. "He has a point. Besides, unless you have a flashlight, you can't be sure what kind of wildlife you might be stepping on."

I look pointedly at her bare feet. She is oblivious to my gesture.

"I saw one time, this show where these mama turtles came up and laid hundreds of eggs in the sand. I'd be sad if I accidentally stepped in a mama turtle's nest."

Bless her. "Yes, it would be the worst."

Sonia's eyes open wider. "Wouldn't it be? I would never be able to forgive myself."

Thankfully the elevator doors open. I step out and wait for her lead.

"I almost forgot." Sonia pulls a plastic card from her back pocket. "This is your key. We're in room 1713."

"Double prime," I mumble to myself as I follow Sonia.

She shoots me a sideways smile. "Trent said the same thing.

What do y'all mean?"

I start to explain and catch myself. "It's a doubly lucky room. That's all."

Sonia offers me a nod of satisfaction. "Only the best for us princesses, right?"

I better win a truckload of cash this weekend. Lord knows I'm going to earn every penny.

Sonia stops and waits in front of room 1713. We stare at each other for a moment, her expression expectant. I raise my eyebrows.

"Try your card out, silly. I know mine works," she says.

I unlock the door and hold it open for Sonia. Following her in, I immediately see a problem. "One bed?"

"A king size," Sonia says as she launches herself into the air. She bounces on impact.

Trent at least has enough common sense to appear chagrined. "When I made the reservations, this was all they had left." He points. "The sofa pulls out into a bed."

Sonia waves her hand. "You don't want to sleep there, April. Those pull-outs are like sleeping on a chain-link fence. This bed is divine."

I was nearly prepared to sleep on the ratty sofa at my sorority house earlier in the day. A pull-out bed at a four-star hotel surely isn't going to hurt me. I pull the cushions off the pull-out.

Sonia props up on her elbows. "Come on, April. Don't be a party pooper. It won't be the first time we've had another girl in our bed. And we both find you attractive."

I glance from Sonia to Trent for confirmation of what I heard. My earlobes feel like someone is holding a cigarette lighter flame to them.

Trent shrugs as he blushes, too. "It was only a phase. We were both curious."

"Playtime isn't part of the bargain," I say. A nervous laugh escapes me.

Trent raises his hands in surrender. "Nope. Your part was to drive us here."

"Come on, April. This bed is way better than a pull-out." Sonia is not going to give up.

"I'm fine." I give the handle of the bed a pull. Nothing happens.

Trent reaches for the grip. I step to the side and mean mug him.

"I'm trying to help," he claims as he pulls the handle. The bed comes open after a momentary strain. Trent flips the bottom half down and points toward the front door. "There are some pillows and blankets in the closet on the left."

I have not felt this awkward in years. Sonia's proposition caught me totally off guard.

"You're really not going to sleep with us?" Sonia whines.

"Sonia, baby. Let it go. You're making her uncomfortable," Trent says.

As I tuck the sheets and blanket on my bed, Sonia continues. "Well, if you change your mind. Come on in."

"Thanks. But I think I'll be fine." I retreat to the bathroom to change into a T-shirt and shorts I plan to use as pajamas.

I'm not a prude. At least, I don't think I am.

It makes no difference to me what Sonia and Trent do in the privacy of their own bedroom. That sort of thing never concerns me about people. Now, if it *includes me*, we have a whole different matter.

When I come out of the bathroom, the lights are off except for the lamp by the sofa. I try to find my bed without looking at Trent and Sonia. I still notice them embracing in my periphery as I flick the light off.

The pull-out is like lying on a chain-link fence with a piece of foam set on top. It squeaks horribly when I make the slightest movement. I try my best to lie perfectly still.

The quiet of the night engulfs me, only to be replaced by the hum of the small refrigerator and AC wall unit in our room. The noise grows, and I realize that I'm wired no matter how tired I am. My body vibrates with nervous energy.

The air in the room is thick, like a highly charged ozone cloud. Something has the energy of the room in a tizzy.

I consider opening my mind to find out what has the energy

swirling. I know better. Whenever I open my thoughts, it's like throwing a door open during a windstorm. There's always a chance I might not be able to close it again.

But my curiosity always gets the best of me.

I lower the partitions in my mind. I take care not to drop them too fast in case I need to slam them shut.

I hear the murmur of gargled voices similar to what I heard while crossing the casino parking lot. An orb of silver mist the size of a softball appears in the right-hand corner of the ceiling. I blink hard to make sure it's not my eyes playing tricks on me.

Regardless of my blinking, the mist remains. I sense no energy from it, nor does it move. Odd on both counts.

Against my better judgment, I continue to lower my partition. I can discern the tone and inflection of each voice right down to the heavy Southern drawl of one and Creole from another. Still, they talk in excited tones and speak over one another.

I realize I have lost track of time. Dawn must be coming soon. No, the morning sun will not dissipate the ghosts. It will, however, make them a lot less spooky.

If I lower my defenses more, I might understand what the spirits discuss. I want to, but I don't dare expose myself any further with the entity residing on the ceiling.

In my experience, spirits who don't readily show themselves fall into one of two categories. Half are too weak or shy, and the others lie in wait until you are fully exposed. I'm not in the mood for having to force an unwanted spirit out of my mind.

Over the drone of the AC, the refrigerator, and the spirits' voices, I begin to hear a wet, smacking noise growing in pace and volume. I concentrate on identifying the sound. I nearly wet the bed when a high-pitched gasp emanates from the other side of the room.

For heaven's sake. Can't those two knock it off for a couple of nights?

Sonia moans louder. I guess I have my answer.

I push the partition back into place, roll over, and pull a pillow on top of my head to cover the lovemaking sounds coming from their bed.

The slapping body noises continue to intensify as the whack of the headboard against the wall joins the lovemaking concerto. This isn't working. I roll onto my back as I pull the pillow off my head and glare into the darkness.

As if me giving them the evil eye in the dark will make them stop.

The silver mist glows brighter, feeding off the energy, I'm sure. To my dismay, it lights the room. In addition to listening to a B-grade porno, I'm greeted with the vision of Sonia's bony butt bouncing up and down on Trent's lap.

Yep. I'm done with this homemade porno.

I clear my throat as loudly as I can as I sit up. "Hey, y'all. I'm going to turn the light on. I'm hungry, and I need to get something to eat."

Sonia flattens against Trent's chest. Trent grips the sheet pulling it up to cover them.

I turn the light on since all body parts which need to be covered are under a sheet. "Sorry. I need to find my sandals."

"No trouble," Trent answers. His voice sounds constricted.

I reach for my purse and check for my door card. "Y'all want anything while I'm out?"

Trent grunts and pushes Sonia off his chest. "I'd like some Skittles. Let me find my wallet."

I momentarily freeze as he throws back the sheets and gets out of bed. He starts to walk to the writing desk without a stitch of clothing.

"No. I got it. My treat," I say as I hurry to the door, diverting my eyes from Trent.

"You sure?" he asks.

"Positive." I nearly break a finger as I run into the door on my way out.

Chapter 6

Alright. I guess I am a prude. I will never be comfortable walking around nude in front of someone I met earlier that morning.

Being hungry is a ruse to let me out of the room. But as the elevator takes its sweet time up to the seventeenth floor, I realize I could use a snack.

A two-pound chocolate candy bar, to be exact.

When was the last time I had sexy time? I'm experiencing an incredibly long carnal-pleasure drought if I need to search my memory this long.

I step into the elevator as I recall the last guy I dated seriously was Mark Hodges, my senior year of undergraduate school. No. Now I remember, we never had sex. A lot of heavy petting, but we never went the whole distance. In hindsight, I'm glad. I would have regretted having sex with him.

I'm not going to let it bother me. Sonia is seven years my junior and probably has already had more sexual encounters than me. I have been busy meeting my goals. But things on the sexual front are about to change colossally.

When I arrive in Atlanta, I will spend a few weeks getting acclimated to my job. Afterward, I plan to date three men a week until I find Mr. Right. Once I find Mr. Right, I will have toe-curling sex for six months straight, every night. Well, every other night.

There is an excellent plan.

I don't understand why I was so worried earlier about not having a plan. Fresh ideas are popping into my head left and right now. I have an idea of how I will earn my rent money and how I will catch up on my sexual encounters.

When the elevator doors open, my attitude is worlds better. I can feel the positivity lifting my spirits.

I exit right and walk down the hallway. I don't remember much from when we arrived, but I recall a snack bar across from the decorative fountain.

It's not much. It consists of only a tiny cubby hole with six tables huddled around a short counter and two glass refrigerators. I'm thankful to find a cashier on duty at this late hour.

"Can I help you?" the short, stocky man asks as I approach.

"Hi. Do you have any cupcakes?"

His face screws up. "This is a snack bar, sweetie. Not a bakery."

I'm not positive, but I'll consider that to be a no. "Sorry. I wanted something sweet other than candy."

"I do have sweet buns. If I warm them up in the microwave, we can agree to call them cupcakes."

I like the way this man thinks. "Sweet buns work for me."

He disappears through a small door to the side of some shelving stocked with candy bars and chips. He reappears, carrying a sweet bun the size of a frisbee in both hands. "You're going to love this. You'll want to buy milk to wash it down."

"Coffee?"

He starts the microwave. "I put a pot on a few minutes ago. If you don't need some fancy brand. This is the standard joe. But it'll put hair on your chest."

I ignore the dad joke I must have heard a million times. "Sounds awesome." I favor him with a grateful smile.

We complete our transaction, and he disappears through the small opening covered with gold plastic strips as quickly as he had appeared. I gather my snack and head to the far table.

I ignore the cacophony of faint voices making it over my mental wall. The speech is louder and more active in the lobby than in our hotel room, but on the positive there is no glowing silver orb in the cafe.

It's a little past four in the morning. Well past the witching hour.

That's an inside joke my brother Dusty and I came up with back when we were messing around in haunted houses in our youth. Ghosts don't care what time it is.

Think about it. Ghosts are caught in purgatory. Time is meaningless to them.

What isn't meaningless to them is the opportunity to communicate with the living. Someone who can hear and see them.

My ability to communicate with them is why I'm so popular with the dead folks when I enter a room. Believe me, it's a type of popularity I would rather do without.

I pull my phone from my back pocket and swipe through the contacts. There are very few people I can call at four AM.

My finger settles over my brother Chase's number. Chase is a crackerjack card player, and he can set me straight on what my plan of action should be tomorrow. Trent says I should stay away from the slots and only play blackjack. But I don't have history with Trent, and I need to be positive since I only have forty-plus dollars to my name.

Who am I kidding? I'm lonely out of my mind, and I need to hear a familiar voice.

"Hello?"

"Chase?"

"Hey, you. What's up?

"Did I wake you?" I ask.

"No … what time is it anyway?"

I slide lower in my seat. "About four in the morning."

"Whew. I must've lost track of time."

"What are you doing?"

He blows a breath into the receiver. "Chief Joe's pickup truck lost all compression. I've been working on it for a couple of days now. I'm afraid it's plumb wore out."

Chief Joe owns four hundred acres of the most godforsaken, rocky, mountain property in Marshall County. He claims to be a descendant of the old Cherokee tribe who once inhabited Alabama. He must be pushing ninety now.

"Are you talking about the truck or Chief Joe now?"

Chase laughs. "The truck. Chief Joe changed his lifestyle after his heart scare last year. Doc Spencer told him no more fried food or candy. He complained about it for a while, but his health has improved. Unfortunately, the truck, I'm afraid I will have to re-bore the engine for him."

"Sounds like a lot of work, Crazy Beaver." I smile when I say it.

"You know I hate that," he grouses.

"Re-boring the truck engine or your Indian name?"

"I don't mind working on the truck for him. He has done a lot for me over the years, and I still go turkey hunting on his property each year."

My brothers and I were hunting on Chief Joe's property when Chase earned his Indian name. We were crossing a small creek a beaver had dammed. Chase inexplicably decided to pull a log off the dam. A rabid beaver charged out and ran Chase hard for at least a quarter of a mile before turning around and heading back to its home.

Chase reported to Chief Joe there was a crazy beaver on his property. Chief Joe laughed so hard he choked and turned blue, which was scary. Once he caught his breath, he proclaimed Chase's Indian name to be Crazy Beaver.

While Chase's name is embarrassing and requires explaining, I love the Indian name Chief Joe gave me. He calls me Hummingbird Fights.

I believe fourteen years have passed since I visited my friend, Chief Joe. When I reached puberty, and the voices began to intensify, he took such an intense interest in me that it made me uncomfortable. He would tell me I needed to embrace the powers I was gifted.

It was easier to stop visiting him.

"Don't you have to open the marina in the morning?" I ask.

"Jenny and Wilson will be there. They can open the marina for me. What gives anyway? Why are you up this late?"

I cross my arms. "I went with some friends down to Biloxi, and I want to try my luck at gambling."

Chase guffaws. "Well, I hope you set a budget. That's the first rule for all gamers."

I think about the forty-five dollars remaining in my wallet. "Oh, I've definitely set a hard stop on the budget."

"Attagirl. The most important thing is to think about it as entertainment and not worry if you lose everything you budgeted. It's about having fun, right?"

Not exactly. "But if you have a small budget, what's the best strategy to allow you to play the longest?"

He pauses. "Some folks like the slots. But personally, they bore me. I would suggest starting out slow at the blackjack table. You'll need to be patient—sorry, not exactly your strength, Tink—and keep the bets small. If you become bored with blackjack, the craps table can be a hoot.

"But if you do craps, promise me not to get caught up in the excitement. I want you to play the pass line, and whatever you do, stay away from the proposition bets."

I have no clue what Chase is talking about, but the inflection of his voice makes me act like I am taking his advice to heart. Lesson number one on effectively communicating with my brothers. If I don't care to get bogged down in minutiae that I couldn't care less about hearing, I have to fake understanding. "Thanks. I'm glad you warned me."

Chase continues to talk about the probabilities at the craps table. Instead, my attention is drawn to a young lady taking a seat at the far booth. She is dressed in a red, white, and blue silk jumper suit and red platform shoes, and her strawberry-blonde hair is pulled into a jaunty ponytail. If it were not so blasted hot outside, I would swear she is dressed for a Halloween party. She would win the best costume prize since she is a ringer for Geri of the Spice Girls.

I stare a little too long at her, making eye contact. Her eyes are crystal blue, highlighted expertly by extensive eyeliner and gunmetal-grey eye shadow.

Her brow pulls together in thought. She stands and starts toward me. Fantastic, crazy white girl coming to ask me what I'm staring at.

"Chase, I'm going to have to let you go," I interrupt him in mid-sentence.

"Oh, sure. Is everything alright?"

"Yeah," I drawl.

A well-put-together man in a dark blue suit appears from the left and intercepts the Spice Girl look-alike. He takes her by the elbow. She tries to pull away but is unable to break his iron grip.

"Well, I'll send you some links on the odds so you can be prepared tomorrow," Chase says in closing.

"You can't be here. You're bothering the customers," the muscular bald man in the blue suit says.

I'm mesmerized by what is unfolding in front of me.

Spice Girl leans in toward the man and says through clenched teeth, "It's a free country, Brodie. I can go where I want."

You tell her, girl. I like the fight in this flyweight.

The man regrips his hand and encircles her tiny arm, lifting her up a few inches as he snaps her arm to the side. I cringe. That will be sore in the morning.

If it hurts, she doesn't let Brodie have the satisfaction of knowing.

"Your type isn't welcome here," Brodie growls at Spice Girl.

"April?"

I had forgotten about Chase. "Sorry, there's a little commotion here." I stand to follow the two outside as Brodie, in his snug blue suit, perp walks Spice Girl out of the casino.

"Are you all set?"

"Yes. Thank you for the info and the links. It'll be helpful, Chase."

"No worries. Be careful and have fun."

"I will." I slide my phone into my back pocket and pick up my pace to catch up with the odd couple.

Chapter 7

I pass the front desk as the sliding doors open for them. They turn left once outside the door, momentarily disappearing from my view. I jog through the glass doors.

They are gone.

I scan the parking lot from left to right. The crisp, salty air lifts my hair, and once again, my nostrils fill with the distinct smell of decay.

This is odd. People don't disappear into thin air.

Refusing to leave the mystery unexplained, I walk between the cars parked in the lot. I freeze as I near the edge of the frontage road and spot a small silver orb of mist traveling down the sidewalk to my left.

I start toward it and reconsider. *You have plenty on your plate already, April May Snow.*

Reluctantly I leave the mystery for someone else to solve and head back into the hotel. I buy a bag of Skittles for Trent and make my way to our room.

Inexplicably they are both sleeping the sleep of the dead. The door handle slips from my fingers. I can't catch the heavy metal door before the spring slams it into the doorjamb. I pivot quickly and look at the bed with my teeth showing from trepidation. Trent and Sonia remain sound asleep.

I give a derisive grunt. Of course, the lovebirds are asleep.

I vaguely recall that elusive, warm, satiated sleep I could occasionally capture with a partner.

Squishing down my envy, I sit on my paper-thin mattress. The chain link below groans as I take off my sandals.

The silver mist has disappeared from the ceiling. That makes sense, I suppose, since I saw it outside.

No. It makes no sense that it was in the room earlier, and then it was outside. It is no more logical than Spice Girl and Brodie disappearing into thin air when I was right behind them.

And where would Brodie have gone? He is a security guard. I should have passed him after he got her out of the casino.

Forget it. It's all making my head hurt something fierce.

I stand, unconcerned about the racket my pullout bed makes, and lay the candy on Trent's nightstand on my way to the bathroom to brush my teeth.

With the sugar coating stripped from my teeth, I turn out the light and climb onto the metal wire torture chamber referred to as a bed. It doesn't matter. I slide into sleep seconds later.

It takes everything I have to wake up the following day. Both Sonia and Trent are freshly showered and bubbling with energy as they convince me to roll out of bed.

I had come to believe the energy level in the hotel had quieted since Brodie, the security guard, chased Spice Girl out of the lobby. I was wrong. There is a steady hum of voices and a swirling of energy while I take a quick shower. If there is this much commotion in our little room, I can only imagine how virile the power will be downstairs.

"Thank you for the Skittles," Trent says as I come out of the bathroom with a denim skirt and T-shirt on.

"You're welcome. Hey. If you want to go on down, I can catch up with you."

"No chance. Take your time. We're in no hurry," Trent says.

I can tell by his nervous energy, Trent is not telling the truth. He is being kind, and it makes it easy to like him.

I'm also warming up to him because he is a man of his word. He pays for all three of us when we enter the breakfast buffet line. The buffet selection is better than I predicted, and I'm strangely famished for some odd reason.

Trent and Sonia do a double-take at the stack of food on my plate.

"What?" I ask a little too combatively.

Neither makes a comment. Smart kids.

"So, where are you two headed this morning?" I ask to divert their attention from my gluttony on display.

"Straight to the poker tables," Trent says. "Did you make up your mind?"

"I plan to take your advice and start out at the blackjack table."

"I'm so excited." Sonia is not joking. She is practically vibrating. "I can't wait to buy a beautiful engagement ring with the winnings. It will be the first thing my grandmother ever did for me."

I stop in mid-bite of a mound of eggs. "What do you mean?"

Sonia purses her lips. "The only reason we have any money to be down here is because of my grandmother Tillie dying."

The empathy gushes out of me as I think about my two grandmothers. I would be horribly heartbroken if I lost either of them. "Oh, Sonia. I'm so sorry."

She hooks a long lock of hair behind her ear. "Don't be. She was a mean old drunk. I'm actually surprised she had anything to leave anyone at all."

I scrutinize Trent. A red rash spreads up his neck. "Seed money for Sonia's future. There are many things she would like to do in her life. Unfortunately, a lot of them require money. Much more than her grandmother left her," he says.

That intrigues me, and I focus on Sonia for further information about her plans.

She, too, blushes as she inspects her hands. "I'm sort of playing around with the idea of going to business school. I have always wanted to own my own business and be my own boss. I think I would love to run either a daycare or a children's art center."

I'm surprised. "Have you ever run an art center?"

"No. But I think I would like it."

Trent leans forward. "She is being modest. Sonia has taken care of her nieces and nephews hundreds of times, and one of their favorite things they do together is art projects. She has a unique skill set of patience with people and an artistic flair."

"You don't necessarily have to go to college to run a business. One of my brothers is remarkably successful in running a marina. He has never had any formal education past high school," I say.

"And he is good at it?" Sonia asks.

"I've always heard making money in business means you're good at it, and the family Marina makes money."

"Interesting. If there is any way I can open a business and not have to go to college, that would be awesome. Not all of us can be smart enough to have colleges trying to recruit us to the math department."

"You are plenty smart in your own ways, baby," Trent says as I hear him pat her leg beneath the tabletop.

"Tell me about this recruiting, Mr. Hotshot."

"Aw, it's no big deal. It was only a couple of schools. Georgia Tech and Michigan were the two major ones who offered a full ride out of state. But I decided on Alabama to stay close to my girl."

As I observe the two interacting, I wonder if this is how Mama and Daddy were when they were young. They, too, met at an incredibly early age, and their families disapproved. They were from two totally different Guntersville cliques. It wasn't precisely the Montagues and Capulets. Still, plenty of ill will and innuendos spread before the two married.

My parents are thicker than thieves, intelligent, and resourceful. The haters never stood a chance of breaking them up.

I might have judged Sonia and Trent's relationship a little harshly to start. They certainly have strong empathy for each other, and their individual goals have become melded into a couple's mission.

Trent places his napkin on his plate. "I can't eat another bite."

I smile at his little white lie. "I'm sure you are champing at the bit to try your hypothesis out. Don't let me keep you."

"Are you sure? We can wait," Trent says.

"I insist. I'm almost done here anyway, and we will be playing different games."

Trent shrugs a shoulder as he stands. "Well, I'm going to take you up on that." He pulls Sonia's chair back for her. "Make a killing, April."

"You too," I reply.

Chapter 8

I'm relieved as they leave. It is not the first time I have drawn conclusions about people before understanding them.

My granny, the zealot, has always preached to me, "Judge not lest ye be judged." It's excellent advice. Unfortunately, it is not always the easiest to follow.

Again, my eyes are bigger than my stomach. I attempt to conceal how much food I have left on my plate. I consider snatching a couple of biscuits and storing them in my purse for a back-up lunch but decide to think positive. I will be buying a prime rib and lobster lunch off my winnings.

Speaking of winnings, I pull out my phone and hit the attachment Chase texted me last night. I scan the cheat sheet for a few seconds and feel like I'm reviewing a calculus problem. "If this then that, but if this then that—" For crying out loud, it's a card game. It can't be so difficult.

The first niggle of doubt slips into my mind. This isn't as good of an idea as I initially thought. Truthfully, this must be the stupidest idea I have had in years.

What was I thinking?

No, this one's not on me. This is Granny and all her manifestation bull malarkey. I got sucked in at a moment of weakness. Yep. I wanted Granny to be right so something would bail me out of my dire financial calamity.

I stare at the leftover cold, yellow scrambled eggs on my plate as if they will reveal the secrets of life. I shake myself out of my trance. Screw it. I only have forty-something dollars. It's not like I'm gambling the down payment on my house.

Walking out of the cafeteria, the surge of paranormal energy coursing through the air slams into me. The hum of multiple conversations plays out in my mind.

This doesn't surprise me. It's easier to keep my mental partition up when I am confident. As I walk to the casino's game hall, I am anything but assured, and my gut is twisting tighter.

As I approach the gilded archway leading into the gaming hall, the voices continue to intensify. I stop and lean against the arch as I fight to catch my breath and clear my mind.

Peering into the high-ceilinged room, I see rows of colorful slot machines. Most of the slots have someone perched on stools like a humanoid vulture waiting intently on the reveal of their spin.

The clatter and ringing of the machines are louder than I remember. The bodiless voices droning in my head roar over the noise of the casino. I consolidate my concentration and focus my energies inward.

This is the first step in regaining control and pushing the partition back in place. My heart rate slows, and my breathing approaches normal as I begin to center myself.

The voices grow quiet, and a gaunt man with an elongated face and spiked, dirty-blond hair approaches the casino hall entrance. I can't explain it; my eyes are drawn to the unkempt man.

His body flickers. It's like looking at an old fluorescent light bulb in the last throes of life. I jerk back with shock.

He notices my reaction. Our eyes lock as he marches toward me, his body oscillating in and out of clarity.

"I see you, and you see me." He cups his hand around his mouth. "I have a secret."

The apparition is casting off an elevated level of excited energy force as he moves into my personal bubble. The putrid scent of feculent red clay and plant decay flows from his mouth. My stomach roils from the stench.

His wild eyes grow huge as he runs a pale hand through his unruly hair. "It's fantastic. It's finally going to happen."

Ghost boy is crazier than an outhouse rat.

I think I might hurl. Tiny beads of sweat pop up on my scalp as I grasp the side of the archway and lean my back against the entrance. Slowly, my vision begins to close in, and I panic that I may be passing out.

"Go away," I croak.

"Are you all right, miss?"

I turn to the concerned-sounding voice. A tall, slender man, about my grandmothers' age, leans in toward me.

I fan my face with my hand. "I think I stood up too fast after breakfast."

His bushy, silver eyebrows come together. "Can I get you something to drink?"

"No. I'll be fine." I'm already feeling better. "I just need to get to the blackjack tables and sit down."

"At least let me help you to the table."

It is illogical, but I'm inexplicably horrified. "Oh, no. I can do it myself."

"No, I insist," he says as he gently props his warm, soft palm under my right elbow. "It's a few steps over there. Still, I can't have you falling out on the floor."

I don't think there is any more concern about me falling out on the floor as the worst of the dizziness passed as soon as the crazy, decayed-breath guy got out of my bubble. Still, I suppose it's better to be safe than sorry, and I don't want to cause an elderly man to worry needlessly.

"What is your name, young lady?" my escort asks as he leads me past the many rows of slot machines.

"April."

He laughs, which draws my eyes to him. I realize he must have been strikingly handsome as a younger man.

"Seriously? You are laughing at my name?"

"No," he drawls. "My name is August."

"You're making that up."

He raises two fingers on his right hand. "Scout's honor."

"Well, I'm not sure I have ever met an August before."

"I know I have never met an April I didn't like." When our eyes meet, he adds, "It's my favorite time of year."

Yea. Dad jokes from the doting grandfather figure. But he is kind, so I'll let it slide.

August gestures to a stool as we approach a blackjack table. "Why don't you take first base. Would it bother you if I play at this table, too?" he asks.

Sort of. "The more, the merrier, I suppose."

Our dealer is close to my age and named Tom. His black, wavy hair is slicked back severely with shiny gel. The faint, wispy mustache on his lip gives him a cartoonish villain appearance. He appears bored as August and I take the two stools next to a middle-aged couple already at the table.

I lay my two twenties down, painfully aware this leaves me only five dollars in my purse. Tom lifts my twenties and sets four blue chips down.

"Oh, I wanted five-dollar chips," I blurt.

Tom tilts his head. "It's a ten-dollar minimum table."

"Ten dollars!" I catch myself as Tom wakes from his state of boredom. "Right. Of course." I gather my composure.

August leans over and whispers. "There is only one casino in town offering a five-dollar table."

"I guess I should have played the slots." I set down one of my four chips.

August frowns. "Slots are for suckers. It's an expensive version of television."

Tom deals me two cards, a two of spades and a three of diamonds. Are you kidding me? It will take me all weekend to get to twenty-one at this rate.

Tom does not wait to ask when it is my turn before he lays the third card down for me.

The Jack of diamonds takes me to fifteen. I try to remember the cheat sheet Chase gave me, and I can't recall a strategy for fifteen. I think it is the card equivalent of no man's land.

Tom raises his eyebrows expectantly. "Hit or stand?"

Good question. I feel I should hold, but fifteen sounds low. "Hit me." The words fall out of my mouth before I can stop them.

Tom flips a card over onto my stack. The ten busts me, and Tom deals August his next card.

It's like being punched in the throat. In one second, twenty-five percent of my cobbled-together money is gone, and the vinyl cover of my stool is still cool on my butt. This is not part of the plan.

No problem. I have three more chances, and the odds must be in my favor. I had a cold start, nothing to worry about here.

I place another blue chip in the rectangular bet outline.

Tom slides me a jack and a king. I'm so excited I can hardly wait for Tom to finish dealing out the rest of the cards.

"I assume you're standing?" Tom asks.

"Absolutely."

"That's a winning hand," August whispers to me as he gestures for another card.

The adrenaline rush is so high that I lean forward in anticipation when Tom reveals his face-down card. I just know I will soon be back to my whole forty dollars. When the ace of hearts pairs up with his ten of clubs, it knocks the wind out of my celebration.

Things just got serious.

On the next hand, I play it safe and hold on to a nine and eight. Tom must draw a card on sixteen and draws a four. I'm devastated, and I'm down to my last chance.

August exhales. "We are not faring too well here."

I had forgotten he was next to me. "I really think I should have stuck with the slots."

"Sorry about my poor advice." August's voice is apologetic.

"Oh, no. It was my brother's idea to play blackjack."

Tom taps the table. "Are you two still playing?"

Losing is more like it. "Sure," I say as I lay my last blue chip on the felt.

Tom gives me my cards. I sit on an eighteen, and Tom has a king showing. Of all the stinking luck.

As Tom flips his face-down card, it's a five. He busts on the next card he draws. August lets out a celebratory holler. It takes me a moment to realize I won my first hand.

This feels awesome. See, this card thing is not tricky at all.

August and I continue our run of good luck for the next thirty minutes. He coaches me on doubles, splits, and surrenders.

We swap to the twenty-five-dollar minimum tables, and our luck continues to hold. I'm now playing with three hundred dollars of house money.

"August Lamar Reeves, I have been looking for you everywhere."

August and I turn on our stools. A strikingly gorgeous woman with gunmetal-colored hair glares at me as she addresses my card mentor. "Did you forget you promised to take me shopping this morning?"

August laughs. Never a wise reaction to a woman who is shooting daggers out of her eyes. I wonder if August is as bright as I thought.

"Now, Trudy. You know I always keep my promises," August says as he slides off his stool.

"Vows too, I hope." Trudy purses her lips as she scowls at me pointedly.

For some dumb reason, my face flushes. "We're playing cards."

August laughs again as he takes hold of Trudy's hand. Yes, he is certainly not real bright. "Trudy, I would like you to meet my friend April. April, my beautiful wife, Trudy."

"Please to meet you, ma'am." I extend my hand, and it hangs in the air.

"I'm sure." She turns her attention back to August. "The stores are already open, and you promised."

"Yes, I did." He favors me with a broad smile. "You are flying solo now, Miss April. I wish you all the luck and happiness in the world."

"Thank you, August." "Thank you" feels inadequate considering how vital his moral support and timely instruction has been, but nothing comes to mind to truly express my gratitude. "You, too."

As August and Trudy walk out of the casino holding hands, I suddenly feel alone. I'm curious about Trent's poker playing, but I don't want to leave the blackjack table while my luck is still holding out.

Chapter 9

I reclaim my stool and am the only person at the table for the next few hands. "Are you from around here, Tom?" Suddenly, I feel the need to make small talk.

"No," he answers as he flips his card over, revealing a sixteen, forcing him to draw. Again, he busts, and I win.

"Hattiesburg?" I ask as he deals me two queens, which I split.

"Baton Rouge." Tom deals me two more cards, an ace on one of the queens and a nine on the second. His lips thin into a narrow line as he flips his card.

"Are you a tiger's fan?"

Tom deals another card to his stack. Oh goody. With a fifteen showing, he will have to draw another card. He closes his eyes as he struggles to maintain his calm, patient facade.

"I have to take my break after this hand," he says abruptly.

His announcement draws my eyes from the table momentarily. Tom's expression turns into one of complete disgust.

"For the love of Pete." Without another word, Tom flips me two more chips, lifts his tray from the table, and leaves me sitting at the table by my lonesome.

Well, how rude.

I'm stunned as I watch Tom walk toward the pit boss. It's not fair Tom can decide to up and leave because I'm having an excellent run of good luck.

The adrenaline from winning wanes, and I count my chips. Fifty blue equals five hundred dollars. Butterflies flutter wildly in my stomach. Not a bad take considering I only brought forty dollars to the table.

But now what?

Briefly, I consider taking my chips to one of the other tables. It's not like there is a shortage of dealers who don't have the sudden need to take a break. But Tom's abrupt departure has put a dent in the winning psyche I have been feeling for the past hour. The last thing I need to do now is foolishly waste my cash windfall.

Tom is right. I could use a break myself. I'm thirsty, and I will be hungry before too long. Besides, I need to find Sonia and Trent to get an update on their progress.

I gather up my chips and slide down from my stool. Now, which way would the poker tables be? I didn't see them on the path in, so they must be further toward the back of the casino.

The high I experienced during the game continues to dissipate. The voices become louder and more garbled in my head as it does. It is unfathomable how much residual emotion can stay in this one room.

Residual emotions are not all that remain. I notice one slot machine has empty seats on either side of it. This is for a disturbing reason: the four-hundred-and-fifty-pound—left arm hugging a family-sized potato chip bag—ghost positioned on the stool of the center slot machine. His spectral girth overlaps onto the adjoining high tops. Any live customer wanting to play those spots would surely experience a cold draft as the hairs on the back of their neck stand up.

The warnings about gambling being a dangerous vice, I always thought to be about destroying your finances. The longer I spend here, the better I understand the reward of endorphins when winning warps your mind. It may be less about the money and more about the hormone secretion.

Heck, I was ready to throttle Tom when he interrupted my perfect game. Now I have a mighty itch to pop some coin into a slot machine and give it a whirl.

As a matter of principle, I march past the last slots without playing a single dollar to prove I can control my urges. Sure, I only manage this by looking straight ahead and concentrating on what sandwich I might want later, but I make it through.

There are more poker tables and craps games than I imagined toward the back of the casino. Most of the craps tables have only a few scattered players, but there is a horde of folks at the poker tables to the right.

Walking toward the tables, I bounce onto my toes with each step to see better over the crowd. I'm obviously not thinking. If Trent is playing, he will be seated, and Sonia is so short I would need a drone flying overhead to locate her.

Table by table, I work my way through the crowd. This is nuts. Who would've ever thought so many people would want to play poker in Biloxi, Mississippi?

My good luck comes back to me as a group of tourists peel away from the table to my right. I catch a quick glimpse of platinum-blond hair. I know my lovebirds have been a pain, but they are my pain, and I feel my face stretch into a smile.

I push my way through the crush of people and tap Sonia on the shoulder. "How's it going, girl?"

She is nibbling at a thumbnail. She turns, and her expression brightens. "April! I'm glad you're here."

"Is everything all right?"

"I hope so." She points to the table. "This game is down to Trent and Sunglasses."

"Sunglasses?" I say with a grin.

She giggles. "I just named him that."

I crane my neck to examine the players. Sure enough, a squatty, middle-aged man wearing reflective sunglasses and a Saints ball cap sits across from Trent. Behind Sunglasses, there is a break in the crowd. This doesn't surprise me since a contingent of spirits is gesturing wildly at Sunglasses' hand. In the group of ghostly gawkers is the spiked-hair spirit who approached me earlier.

Spiked Hair locks eyes with me and waves. I wave before I realize it. Splendid, nothing like encouraging him.

"I can't believe there are this many people playing poker," I say.

"I tell you it's meant to be, April. Trent and I were going to Montgomery, and there aren't any tables down there, plus my car died. But you set us straight about the tables and gave us a ride. Now come to find out, this weekend is the Biloxi Queen's annual district poker qualifier. The dealer told us the event draws people from all over the Southeast. Can you believe it?"

On this trip, I'm starting to think I'll believe anything. "Well, we're having a long run of unbelievable luck."

"I know. *Right*?"

"So, I take it his theories are working?"

Sonia resumes gnawing on her thumbnail to the quick. "I think so. He's doing really well."

"How are y'all on money?"

"Not for sure, but there is a crap pile of chips."

I scan the table, taking notice of the monstrous stack of chips in front of Trent and still more enormous mound in the pot. "How much does this game payout?"

Sonia mumbles over her thumb, "I think if he wins this one, he said he wins like forty-five hundred?"

I choke and can't respond. Forty-five hundred? My five-hundred-dollar winnings are chicken scratch in comparison. I don't want to get chip envy, but I can't help but compare Trent's sizable stack and the mound in the pot against my purse's fifty blue chips.

"Well, when Trent wins. Y'all are definitely buying dinner tonight."

She cuts her eyes to me and laughs. "He'll be buying both of us a steak dinner."

"Huge, melt-in-our-mouth steaks."

"Amen."

Mr. Sunglasses is down to a few chips. Still, he wins two more hands before he runs dry on the last hand.

Sonia reaches out and grabs my wrist. I don't mean to, but her energy level is so high from the excitement her feelings dump into me and bring tears to my eyes.

This girl is so in love with her boy that her emotions overwhelm me. Her passion is pure and unconditional. The sort of love that could fix the world if there were more of it.

I'm already rooting for Trent to win, but now it takes on an extra urgency. My friends need this win, and if it helps grow the love she holds in her heart, I want it desperately for them.

"He's going to win," I whisper.

"I hope you're right."

Trent calls the bet. Sunglasses smirks as he lays down three fives.

Sonia sucks in a breath and squeezes my wrist tighter. I lay my other hand over hers.

"You've got this, Trent," I whisper.

Trent lays down a full house. The spectators clap as Sonia jostles me by jumping up and down. I'm so happy. I turn and pull Sonia into an embrace as she stops jumping.

"Oh my gosh, this is exciting," she screams in my ear.

It is. I'm so excited that you would think I won the money for my friends. Trent motions for Sonia as he collects the pot and stands.

"He's calling for you," I say.

Sonia releases her hold on me, wipes a tear of joy from her eyes, and slides through the dispersing crowd to Trent. At first, I don't plan to follow, but then I think, what the heck, I'm part of this little family while we are on our crazy trip together.

"Can you believe it?" Trent hollers as we approach.

"It's incredible!" Sonia shouts.

Trent puts his arms around her, lifting her off her feet as he crushes his lips to hers. He holds her mashed to his chest as he turns twice in a circle. I wonder how long they can hold their breath. As he breaks his kiss from Sonia, he notices me and pulls me into their lovefest. "You made this happen, April."

My face heats from the undeserved praise. I certainly didn't give them a ride to Biloxi out of the goodness of my heart. "No, you did this, Trent."

His attention glides back to Sonia. "No. We would be down in

Montgomery right now and have missed out on all this."

"Do you think it's enough, baby?" Sonia asks.

"Enough to get my beautiful girl an engagement ring," his expression hardens with determination. "But we'll need to win some more to make sure you can open up your art school."

"I love you, Trent."

He kisses her on the lips again. "I love you, baby.

Right about now, I'm feeling incredibly awkward, and I scan the room, looking at nothing in particular. These two are glowing with such love toward one another, I feel voyeuristic watching them kiss. The vision of them making love last night sneaks into my mind, and I wince. I guess there is a genuine reason I should feel like a voyeur.

"Are you hungry, baby?"

"Starving."

Trent pulls out his wallet and hands Sonia a couple of twenties. "You two go get something to eat. Take your time. I can wait a little bit longer, but I'll want something in an hour."

"Why can't you come with us?" Sonia pouts.

"Aww, baby. I have another game starting up in fifteen minutes."

"You can't take a few minutes to eat with us?"

"I'm sorry." He leans in and kisses her on the forehead. "You and April go and enjoy your lunch and let me get back to work."

"All right. Is there any particular sandwich you want?"

"Surprise me like you always do," he says as he turns his attention back to the game table.

"How many games does he have left to play today?" I ask.

"I'm not sure. I hope not many since we still haven't walked on the beach yet."

I'd suggest we find a restaurant on the water and go for a walk, but I'm reasonably sure the allure of walking on the beach has as much to do about Sonia holding hands with Trent as it does the experience of something new.

"Are you okay with getting some sandwiches at the Gold Rush grill?" Sonia asks.

"Sure."

Being with Sonia is like riding a yo-yo. It's amazing how quickly her emotions can change from complete exultation when Trent won to a depression close to despondent when they are separated.

I'm sure having someone totally in love with you at times might be super cool. But it must also be a heavy burden to know you hold such sway over another person's happiness. As much as I think I want their level of commitment and intimacy someday, I think I'm fine being responsible for April right now.

We order our sandwiches with barely a word between us. You would think someone died rather than won enough money for an engagement ring. I don't usually require my friends to entertain me. Still, Sonia's disappointment about Trent not eating lunch with us is causing my attitude to drop, too.

Since there is no conversation, I decide to check my phone. My daddy sent me a text asking how I was doing and if he would see me soon. Ouch, his question hits a little too close to the mark. Depending on how I finish out at the tables will decide for me if I remain independent this summer or if a surprise visit to my parents is in my future. I'll answer him later.

My brother Dusty texted, too. He lets me know he set an appointment at my sorority house to investigate the ghost of Rhonda Riley. He also wants to know how I want him to get the thousand-dollar finder's fee to me.

Score! I forgot about the money I earned from him. With the money I already won, I'm now in striking distance of my eighteen-hundred-dollar goal.

Bless it. Eighteen hundred dollars is my goal if I don't plan to eat all summer. That would only ensure I have a roof over my head.

Why had I not thought of this sooner?

"What are you looking at?" Sonia asks.

"My dad and brother have been texting me."

"Y'all are close. Aren't you?"

Self-conscious, I set the phone down. "I like to think we are."

"You're close with your mama, too?"

"Sure. But if Mama wants me, she usually calls." Or I call her if I'm in an extraordinarily dark place.

Sonia wipes the condensation from her glass of water. "I wish I were close with my mom."

There is nothing I can say to assuage her regret, so I remain silent. Besides, I'm not fond of "sorry for myself" Sonia. I much prefer the wild-eyed, anything-goes version of her.

"You know he is only playing the game to help you open your kids' art school."

Sonia's head snaps back like I slapped her. "I know. But I miss him."

"It's for a little while, Sonia. He's not gone anywhere."

"I don't expect you to understand. I suppose it's different if you have only one person in the entire world who believes in you."

She says it kind and in a whisper voice, yet the words cut me like a knife slashing into my sternum, stealing my breath. It's perfect timing since our server shows up with our sandwiches, saving me from saying anything else stupid.

"I declare. I'm such a bad friend. I forgot to ask you how you did at the blackjack tables."

My winnings are so insignificant compared to Trent's that I am embarrassed. "I've worked my way up to five hundred dollars."

"Awesome," Sonia says.

I check to make sure there is no mustard on my turkey sandwich. "It's a start. And I have learned so much today."

"There's a lot to be said for learning. These card games are really complicated. I'm sure it takes a while to know what you're doing."

"Well, twenty-one isn't overly complicated," I say.

I don't catch what Sonia says next as the skin at the top of my chest tingles as if I were touched by a live wire. Scanning over Sonia's shoulder, I see Spice Girl standing at the doorway under the lighted Gold Rush sign. Her back is to me, and her left hip is cocked as she appears to wait for someone.

"Sonia, do you see the girl in the red-and-blue outfit? " I already suspect she can't. Still, Spice Girl's apparition is so complete there is a chance I might be mistaken.

"What, girl?"

I point toward the diner entry. "Right there. Under the marquee. She's wearing red shorts and a blue-and-white top."

Sonia squints. "I don't see anyone."

"No girl in red platform shoes leaning against the entrance?"

Sonia smirks. "What sort of lettuce did they put on your turkey sandwich?"

As I expected. "Oh, never mind. She's left now."

Sonia has a skeptical expression. "You're crazy." She pops a French fry in her mouth.

If I don't get a hold of my psychic abilities soon, I *may* become mental.

Chapter 10

Sonia orders Trent a club sandwich, and we walk back to the casino together. She peels off right to take Trent his lunch, and I head for the twenty-five-dollar blackjack tables.

The spiked, dirty-blond hair apparition blocks my path. "Going back to the blackjack tables?"

I roll my eyes. "What's it to you?"

"Since we can communicate, I thought we could have a little fun."

"I'm busy," I say as I step around him.

He reappears in front of me and holds out his hands. "Hey, slow down and listen to me."

"What did you say your name is?"

"Alvin." He stands taller. "Alvin Lewinsky."

"Alvin, I'm busy."

"You'll want to hear me out."

Sure. Because every girl needs to hear out a dead man claiming he wants to have some fun with her. Against my better judgment and hoping he will leave me alone afterward, I cross my arms and say, "You've got one minute."

He flashes his rotten teeth. "Now, look. Nobody else in this dump can see me. Well, no live people. So, here's what I'm proposing. I'll read the deck and give you a thumbs up or thumbs down. Thumb up, take a card, thumb down, hold."

"Are you done?" I ask.

"Yes."

"Not interested." I intend to walk around Alvin, but half my body passes through him, causing both of us to give a brief shudder of disgust.

"Aw, come on now. If you ain't cheating, you're only cheating yourself."

I stop dead in my tracks as a chill runs up my spine. Alvin knows precisely which buttons to press to get my attention.

How often have I heard my brother Chase make the same comment, or his second favorite, "If you ain't cheatin', you ain't tryin'"? Chase's hyper-competitiveness often makes him bend the rules to secure a victory. I call it cheating. He calls it giving it all you got.

"Listen, I know you mean well." Or at least I think he does. "But please leave me alone. If I win or lose, I will do it on my own, and I don't need any coaching from you."

"What about if I flash the value of the next card?"

"No! No signaling."

"Can I at least watch you?"

Peaches. "Sure. You can watch but no signaling and especially no talking." I turn and head toward the tables without waiting for his confirmation.

Thirty minutes later, I think I should've taken Alvin up on the help. I've blown through four hundred and twenty dollars.

Alvin, for his part, holds true to his word. He's not said a single thing to me while standing behind the dealer. As for the signaling, his vulgar gestures of disgust with each losing hand can't be considered signaling. Unless he's signaling that I'm an idiot.

There's something profoundly different about this game compared to the game I played with August at my side. Confidence. I'm missing the confidence of knowing I will manifest a win. I'm past the point of thinking Granny's ideas are bull malarkey. I need money, or I'm going to be homeless when my last eighty dollars run out unless there is some truth to her belief.

Honestly, what do I have to lose at this point?

I start to lay down the next chip, hesitate, then gather up my eight chips and step down from the stool. I'm not ready to place the bet yet. I don't believe in Granny's manifestation any more than in the Easter Bunny. At least I don't believe in it right now. I might be able to brainwash myself again given enough time.

You don't know the actual depth of your own stupidity until you are desperate. I'm sure there is a case study on such things in a psychology book somewhere. If there isn't, there should be.

My chest tightens, and it's harder to breathe. My mental barrier falters with my indecision and anxiety, and the plethora of voices again murmur in my head.

Deep breath. Relax. You can't have a heart attack at the age of twenty-seven. Besides, I don't want to explain to Mama why I was at a casino when she visits me at the hospital.

This is such a harebrained scheme. What made me think I could come down here and win money anyway?

A clarifying thought of ingenuity comes to me during my deepest despair. It's a hunch, and I spend the next ten minutes watching the dealer. Specifically, I'm studying the deck and predicting the next card.

The first three cards I miss badly. The fourth card I see in my mind is the jack of diamonds, and it comes up king of diamonds. Both are guys from the diamond family. That's good. Right?

Oh, come on, April. It's a sheer coincidence.

I misread the next card and begin to dismiss the whole idea as hogwash until I realize I read the six backward. It was a nine. An easy enough mistake to make.

Butterflies tingle in my stomach as I understand I'm doing this. I'm reading cards. Sure, it's not perfect, but I have an unfair advantage at this point.

To make sure, I watch three more draws from the dealer. A three of spades I see turns out to be three clubs. As my confidence flags, I envision an eight of diamonds, and the next card played by the dealer is the eight of diamonds. I let out a small whimper of excitement. Everyone turns to me briefly. The third card I see in my mind's eye is a nine of hearts. Again, the upside-down version six of hearts is dealt. I'll have to remember the upside-down thing when I'm betting. Avoid high bets on sixes and nines, April.

I retake my stool. Even though I'm reading the cards, it doesn't remove the anxiety afflicting me. I feel I'm wound so tightly my spring might break. I only have three more plays. This must work.

Alvin stares at me expectantly, and I shake my head. Chase would be mad if he knew I didn't use every edge at my disposal. Heck, I'm not so sure I'm not crazy for refusing Alvin's paranormal assistance. But I feel the need to win on my own.

When my first card is a four, I groan. I'm a fool for believing a trip to the casino is a real plan for coming up with my rent money. I'm obviously calling Daddy for a money wire in a few minutes.

I see my next card clearly in my mind. It's an eight of hearts. As the dealer flips the card onto my deck, I can't hide my grin. First, because my read was correct, but more importantly, it now puts me in an excellent position for twenty-one.

I tap the top of my cards and don't bother to read the next. A Jack lands on the green felt. I leap into the air before latching onto the table's edge to not fall off my stool. Alvin gives me an elevated thumbs up from behind the dealer.

I know it's a twenty-five-dollar bet. But it changes everything.

If the house has a slight advantage typically and wins money every day at this game, surely the slight edge will allow me to earn what I need. I can't feel guilty about it, given how badly I need the money. Besides, the casinos played with an unfair advantage all these years. Why can't I have an unfair advantage for a day?

A few hours later, I'm up a boatload of chips, and I know I'm reading cards beyond any doubt. Alvin is jumping up excitedly, pumping his fist into the air and screaming his joy, but only I hear. I'm in the zone. I'm making it happen and am invincible.

I'm a splitting, doubling and holding, wild card whipping, chip-slinging fool. Time stops and carries no meaning as I show the dealer and the casino who's boss.

Don't get me wrong, I haven't thrown out all caution. I'm purposely losing a hand every five plays, and I've misread a few cards. Stupid sixes and nines. But the errors make my game decisions more realistic and help me keep my advantage undercover.

I know what you're thinking. It's wrong. You might consider it stealing. But by gosh, I need this money, and I'm going to count it as a godsend. It's merely a manifestation of my desires like Granny described.

Plus, it's a huge rush. It's better than any experience I've ever had before.

"You've got to stop now." The cold breath blows into my ear. I jerk to my right. Alvin is in my personal space.

"What?"

"Pit boss." Alvin inclines his head. "He's onto you counting cards."

"I'm not…" Peaches. I almost said "counting cards" aloud.

"Take your chips now, or he will brush you back."

"What?"

Alvin licks his blue lips. "Forget about it. No time to explain. But if you don't pick up your chips now, you'll lose it all."

I'm confused and angry. "He can't do that."

"Go any slower … you're going to experience it firsthand," Alvin warns.

It's not fair. I have a hot hand, and my system is working. A couple more hours, and I'd have my rent money and more to spare. Why should I be disrupted by some overweight, middle-aged man walking around in a suit?

The pit boss scans the blackjack area, and our eyes meet briefly. I quickly avert my eyes and begin to gather my chips reluctantly. Alvin is right. Better to be safe than sorry.

As I pick up the last of my chips, I notice the pit boss walking quickly in my direction. I drop my chips into my purse and head in the opposite direction.

There's enough reflection from mirrors and glass in the casino. When I walk between slot machines, I see the boss following me. Stopping in front of one of the slot machines, I act like I'm interested in playing. I watch him in the reflection of the black glass divider behind the slot.

He slows and stops. I assume to decide what I'm going to do next.

A thought comes to me, and I pull my phone out of my purse and pretend to take a call. I smile broadly and begin to talk as I turn and walk toward the pit boss. I watch him in my peripheral vision, heading toward the cashiers as I pass.

A single bead of sweat traces down my spine as I take the last turn and lose view of him in the reflective wall panels. Alvin appears next to me and lets out an excited howl.

"Whew, I thought you were going to blow it. The pit boss was all about busting you."

I'm all about giving credit where credit is due. "Thank you, Alvin. If you hadn't warned me, I would be in major trouble now."

He waves his hand at me. "Don't mention it. But you wouldn't have been in any trouble. He would have taken your chips and told you you're not welcome to play here anymore."

"Trouble enough, considering how badly I need this money."

"Yeah, it's one thing to lose the money fair and square. It's another thing to have the pit boss take it from you."

I feel a twinge of guilt. Actually, the pit boss would've been in the right since I was basically stealing in my situation. "Well, it wasn't exactly legitimate how I won it since I was reading cards."

Alvin steps in front of me, and I must stop not to walk through him.

"Reading cards?" he asks.

"Sure. How else do you think I was winning?"

Alvin's blue lips purse as his eyebrows draw together. He bursts into laughter.

"What?" I ask.

"That's rich. You thought you were reading cards."

"I was."

He stops laughing but continues to grin. "Nah, honey. I can read cards because I'm dead, but you weren't reading cards."

I thrust my hand into my purse and pull out a handful of the chips. "What do you call these?"

"Good luck. I felt the juices running off you the moment you stepped into the room. You weren't reading cards; you were riding one of the biggest lady-luck surges I've ever felt."

It's not clear to me if Alvin is correct or not. Since I would prefer not to have been doing something illegal, I want him to be telling the truth. "Are you sure?"

"If I'm lying, I'm dying."

We both take the measure of Alvin's present condition. He chuckles and adds, "Well, you know what I mean."

I shake my head at him as we arrive at the cashiers. I pull all the chips out of my purse and push them toward the woman.

"Profitable day," she comments as she counts my chips.

"Luck was on my side today."

"It sure was." She makes an entry onto her pad. "Do you want your payment in cash or check, dear?"

I'm not sure why, but the question sends an electrical thrill through my body. "How much?"

"Four thousand."

I choke and struggle to answer. "Five hundred cash and thirty-five hundred in check, please."

As the pleasant lady counts out five crisp, hundred-dollar bills, I feel off balance. Oblivious to my sudden vertigo, Alvin gives me the double thumbs up next to me.

"You're going to eat well tonight," he says.

"More like have a place to sleep for the summer."

"Pardon?" The cashier peers over her reading glasses.

"Nothing." I wave at her. "I was talking to myself."

She flashes a concerned expression. "Now, make sure to use the safe in your room for your check. If you lose it or if someone steals it, they won't let me cut another one for you."

"Yes, ma'am."

The cashier slides out the cash and lays the blue check on it. The moment is surreal as I push them into my purse.

"Thank you."

She smiles. "Don't spend it all in one place, dear."

Unfortunately, I'll have to, as most of my winnings are earmarked for my apartment's rent. "Thanks."

"You won some big dog dough there, kiddo," Alvin says.

The initial excitement and adrenaline from the winnings wane, and I notice my energy level flagging. I need to lie down and rest in the worst of ways. But there is something I can't leave undone.

"Thank you, Alvin. There's no way I could have won so many hands without your help."

"Help? You wouldn't let me help. You did this all on your own."

I'm still unsure if Alvin is telling the truth or if he gets some supernatural joy from making me think he had no part in my winnings. Either way, I know playing with a partner at the table was more comfortable. It's phenomenal having a personal cheering section, even if they are dead.

"If I did do this on my own, I want you to know I still appreciate your company while I was at the table. I know I wasn't exactly receptive at first."

Alvin raises his eyebrows. "Not receptive? I'd hate to see it when you put your foot down."

I roll my eyes. "Well, I'm trying to be nice now, so don't screw it up. What can I do for you? How can I return the favor?"

Alvin rocks back and gawks at me as if I have lost my mind. "What do you mean?"

It's never any fun to be overly obvious, but I need to settle up with Alvin quickly and get upstairs and rest. I gesture from his feet to his head with my hand. "Well, you're dead."

He chuckles. "I thought we already established my current shortcomings."

"Yes, but you're still here. Is there something I can do to help you move to the next plane?" I make a circular motion with my hand. "You know, be at peace?"

He doubles over as he grabs his gut and laughs uncontrollably. "Be at peace? You're killing me."

"What's so funny?"

"Sorry. I can't wait to hear you say, 'go to the light, Alvin. Follow the light.' That is what you plan to say, isn't it?"

I shrug. "I don't know."

"It is!" He points at me and laughs again.

"I was only trying to be helpful."

He sobers. "I know. And it's sweet of you to offer."

Alvin spreads his arms above his head and turns slowly in a circle. He stops when facing me. "Why would I leave this? I love the constant drama, highs, and lows, the blast of energy from the big-ticket winner, and the bittersweet anxiety of the poor soul who played their last dollar. There is nowhere in this universe with so much emotion packed into one small area. April, I'm already in heaven."

Alvin winks at me, turns, and fades from my view as he strolls toward the casino entrance. There's an odd emptiness coming over me. Although he can be highly annoying, I hope this is not the last time I see Alvin.

Chapter 11

Once I stash my winnings in our room's safe, I lie down on the sofa to take a nap. I'm so exhausted I feel like I haven't slept in weeks.

The room is still humid, but the air conditioning is doing a fair job of cooling the room, and I slip off to sleep.

It's not a deep sleep. It's one of those naps where I'm conscious I'm not in my regular bed, and things are different all around me.

My mind's dark-gray blank screen snaps to a clarified vision, and I'm back on the casino floor. This time I'm not at the blackjack tables. Instead, I'm standing at the craps table. I feel the hard square dice squeezed tightly in the palm of my right hand. People all around the game table are hollering encouragement.

Some are alive and some are ghosts. Each holds an expression of excitement and anticipation. All eyes are on me.

I'm winning again. I feel the same surge of energy I felt while playing cards today.

Could this be a vision? Is this of things to come?

A sudden tightness grips my gut. Something is wrong. Something is terribly wrong.

Is it a bad roll? Should I call it quits and cash in? Is impending bad luck what this is about?

A cracking sound reverberates around and through me. It sounds similar to two green two-by-fours being slapped together in quick succession.

I hear a woman scream and everyone at the table rubbernecks in the direction of the noise. With no warning, I fall back from the dream. No matter how much I try to cling to the memory, it fades out of focus. I try desperately to recapture the vision to learn its meaning and what happened to cause the woman to scream, but it's gone. Mimicking a flash of lightning, the images burn indelibly onto my mind, but the source has dissipated into nothingness.

I open my eyes and remain still. Call it intuition, but I know I needed to stay in the dream long enough to decipher its secrets. I know I will regret not having unlocked its clues quick enough.

The door to the hotel room clicks and swings open. Trent and Sonia enter and pull up short, noticing me on the sofa.

"I'm sorry, April. We didn't know you were sleeping," Trent says.

I push up onto my elbow. "No, I've been up for a while. How did you do?

"He killed it!" Sonia blurts.

"Well, I didn't exactly kill it, but I did have a productive day. That's why we were looking for you. We're headed out to a steakhouse for dinner and want you to come with us."

I pull out my phone and check the time. *It's seven? I must've been more tired than I first thought.* "You sure you two don't want a date night? I'll let you borrow the car."

"Don't be silly," Sonia says. "We're a team, and we need to catch up on how each other is doing."

"Plus, the deal was I pay for dinners. I don't ever like to renege on deals," Trent says.

I can tell by their expressions that they're not just being polite. They are genuine with their invitation, and I realize it would be rude to turn them down no matter how much I would rather be by myself tonight. Being practical, if I don't go, I'll be hunting for a sandwich in only a few hours anyway.

"Give me a few minutes to freshen up."

We pull into Diamond Dave's steakhouse half an hour later. I hand the valet my keys. Hey, I know it's extravagant, but I figure

I can live high on the hog for another twenty-four hours. Besides, Trent is buying dinner.

The host seats us at a well-worn booth at the back of the restaurant. I can't help but think the setting is perfect for a couple on an anniversary date. For the life of me, I can't figure out why Sonia and Trent want a third wheel tonight.

"You two should've come here by yourselves. A romantic dinner for two would have done you good."

Trent smiles. "We have our entire life for dinner alone. This might be the last time the three of us enjoy dinner together."

Why would the last opportunity to have dinner together matter? Also, why did my eyes fill with tears at his statement?

"This road trip has been life-changing for us," Sonia says. "We're glad you shared it with us."

It's difficult to understand how these two, who barely know me, treat me like family. Meanwhile, my sorority sisters turned their back on me this week during my moment of need. The rejection from my sisters still stings, and the pain gnaws on my tender feelings when I remember the phone call to Breanna. I start to ask why they're glad I took the trip with them.

Trent beats me to the punch. "How did you fare at the blackjack tables?"

I welcome the diversion. Talking about my mastery of the blackjack tables will take my mind off of the treachery of my sorority sisters. "I cleared four thousand dollars today."

"Wow! You won more than what you needed for your rent," Sonia says.

"Incredible, April. You had a spectacular day at the blackjack tables," Trent says.

I can't contain my smile as the details gush from me. "I know, right? It's like I got on this roll, and there was nothing but the dealer and me in the world."

"You were in the zone."

Sonia nods in agreement. "Definitely in the zone."

"I was in something. All I know is winning the money made me feel like a goddess."

"It is a true high," Trent concurs.

I gesture to him. "Tell me about your game. I take it by this fancy dinner we're eating, your analytics are working?"

"Mostly." Trent shrugs. "It's not working exactly like I thought it would, but other things are coming into play."

"Other things?"

"It's difficult to explain. There's way more psychology and sociology involved than I imagined. It's not all straight card probabilities, but I'm figuring it out on the fly."

"Figured it out to eight thousand dollars," Sonia announces.

"Dang. And you're making a fuss over my little winnings."

"Everything is relative, April. The money can come quicker in poker. Blackjack winnings take time to build up."

It occurs to me we already exceeded the money goal we hoped to win. Our winnings already surpassed our wildest expectations. The intelligent play is to pack up and head north, singing "Zip-A-Dee-Doo-Dah" the whole way home. Why risk losing our hard-won winnings tomorrow needlessly?

Besides, there's some evil juju floating around the Delta Queen casino. I can't put my finger on it, but I don't want to spend a second longer than necessary. Not all the spirits I'm aware of are as kind and thoughtful as Alvin.

There is also the matter of the unexplained dream I experienced before Trent and Sonia entered our room. I can't understand what the vision foretells, but it's got me as nervous as a long-tailed cat in a room full of rocking chairs. I don't want to be around when its meaning is revealed.

"Let's head home tonight."

Sonia leans back. "You're serious?"

"Yes. I am. We've both won the amount of money we said we needed at the start. Let's not be greedy."

"I understand your point, April, but I'm entered in a game in the morning," Trent says.

"You don't have to play."

He presses his lips tightly together. "Actually, I kind of do. There was a nonrefundable five grand buy-in. If I don't show in the morning, I lose the money."

"Oh."

"There's no one saying *you* have to play tomorrow, April. You can rest in the room until we're done, and then we can head home."

"You could go shopping or something if you want. I can call you to pick us up when we're done," Sonia offers.

I wave my hand at them. "No, don't be silly. It was just a thought. I'm probably being overly conservative."

Chapter 12

We go to bed with hardly a word when we return to the hotel. I lay awake on the sofa bed, wondering if I should have pressed the issue of going home more vigorously. I realize the thought of us losing money is not where my fear originates.

The dream with the loud clapping noise followed by the woman's blood-curdling scream is what gives me the willies. The uneasy feeling I can't shake. In fact, I'm terrified to close my eyes and fall asleep.

I know my fear doesn't make sense, given that I wanted to stay in the dream state to figure out what happens and learn what it all means. But several hours later, I'm convinced what occurred during my dream foreshadows future events, and they are not good.

The day's excitement must have taken a toll on Trent's and Sonia's energy levels. Fortunately for me, there is no porn movie showing in high definition ten feet from the sofa tonight.

There's also no visit from the odd silver orb. It's me and my troubled thoughts in the darkness.

At one in the morning, I finally give in to my restlessness. It's pointless to continue lying on the uncomfortable pull-out bed, staring into the pitch black.

I slip on my sandals and slide silently out our door. As I wait for the elevator, I rub my hands across my face. My body's time clock is all out of whack. That's all. There's nothing truly wrong with me. Much.

The same balding man watches over the coffee counter tonight. As I approach, he breaks into a welcoming smile.

"I thought you might be back tonight."

Odd. "You did?"

"Maybe I just hoped it."

I didn't pick up a creepy vibe from him the night before, but I'd be lying if I said the conversation isn't making me uncomfortable. "Well, here I am."

"Wait a second. I have a surprise for you."

He disappears into the back, and I consider this might be the best time to run back to our room. Forget it. My curiosity has already kicked in, and I now want to see his surprise for me, for better or worse.

When he reappears, he hides his right arm behind his back. "I felt bad last night that I couldn't give you a cupcake, so I got you this."

He offers me the most enormous cupcake I've ever seen. It's a beautiful, softball-shaped chocolate cake with pink icing and delicate lilac sprinkles.

"Oh my. You shouldn't have."

He's obviously happy with my response. "I've been telling the boss we need to expand into pastries for years. But you know how bosses are. They never listen."

"Well, thank you. This is definitely gonna hit the spot tonight."

He turns and pours a cup of coffee and hands it to me. "Well, us sweet tooths have to stick together. Everyone else thinks of spaghetti and meatloaf when you say comfort foods. Me, I prefer a double-helping wedge of German chocolate cake."

"So weird. I like German chocolate, too." It sounds stupid when I say it, but what else was I supposed to say? "How much do I owe you?"

The cashier steps back and holds his hands up. "On the house tonight. But in case you get hit up by management for a survey, remember my name is Leon."

His smile is infectious. "You've got a deal, Leon. And thank you again."

"My pleasure."

Already normalizing to this late-night routine, I sit down in the same booth I was in last night as I begin to savor my cupcake and coffee.

Is there anything that makes you forget your troubles like an oversized cupcake? If for only a few minutes, it's like sugar meditation disconnecting your mind from any worries you carry.

It isn't the best cupcake I have ever had, but it is incredibly fresh and definitely in the top ten. I'm finishing off the last few bites when Spice Girl shows up again.

I'm surprised, although I'm not sure why. I suppose it makes sense she replays the same loop over each night. She wears the same desperate expression as she tries to find a mark for her services.

What happened to her? Why is she stuck in a loop rather than having free rein in this plane like Alvin? I have so many questions, but I also know I'll let sleeping dogs lie if I'm smart.

On cue, she makes eye contact with me. I should look away, and I want to, but I can't. I realize she's considerably younger than I first believed.

Spice Girl starts to walk toward me, and the smartly dressed security guard appears out of thin air intercepting her mere feet from my table. They exchange words briefly before he pins her arm to her back and begins to walk her out of the coffee shop toward the lobby entrance.

I hesitate for a moment. *Let it go, April.*

Not happening. I can't let it go.

I gather up my trash and dump it in the bin, waving at Leon as I exit the coffee shop. "Thank you, Leon."

Only the security guard's back is visible to me as I make it into the lobby. They make a left-hand turn and disappear from my view. Jogging to the front door, I burst through, searching to my left.

They're gone, save for a silver-mist orb floating down the

sidewalk at waist height.

Now what? Follow a supernatural entity down streets I'm not familiar with at two in the morning? That doesn't exactly sound sane.

I start after the silver orb, making sure to stay a few yards behind. It never varies its speed and continues along at the same height.

I'm fortunate that my sandals are ultra-comfortable because I chase after the orb for at least ten blocks. It slides in between the bars of the wrought-iron gate of the city's cemetery, and I feel my stomach sink.

Of course, the ghost is headed to the cemetery. Why would I think anything else?

Cemeteries are problematic for me. There are always so many restless spirits excited to have someone who can communicate with them. They talk over one another more often than not, and I can't make any sense of them.

My resolve wavers since I don't want to deal with a stimuli overload tonight. But I also want to figure out the story behind Spice Girl.

I build the mental wall in my mind and prepare the best I can before pushing against the wrought-iron gate. Curiously, it's not locked. It groans as the ponderous gate swings on rusted hinges.

The silver orb is now out of my sight. I track back to the left, the direction its glow was in view last. I walk as quickly as I dare, pulling out a flashlight from my purse as I go.

My mind shield is strong enough to keep most voices at bay. But there's no shield for my eyes, and this old establishment is full of ghosts too stubborn to release their hold on this world and move on.

Out of respect, I am careful to step over the graves as I go.

The orb blips behind a grotesquely twisted oak tree in the center of the cemetery. I see the silver glow only for a brief second, but I hurry my pace toward the disfigured oak.

Excitement builds in me as I realize I am close. I pick up my pace through the tombstones.

My knee cracks against one of the granite markers, and I double over, grabbing my leg as pain shoots through me. Shaking off the anguish, I limp toward the oak in the center of the cemetery. I hope I haven't permanently lost the orb's trail.

I approach the tree. The odd pattern of the bark, illuminated by the orange moon, appears to resemble faces. I squint my eyes as I study the bark closer. With sudden clarity, I can discern hundreds of faces formed by the ridges in the bark, each watching me intently.

An uneasy feeling tracks through me as I stare at the faces. I check behind me. The iron gate should be in front of me; instead, it is on my left. It's as if the world has rotated on its axis.

Weird. But I have no explanation for it. It's not of immediate importance, so I continue my search.

I step around the massive oak and immediately see Spice Girl sitting on one of the sarcophaguses near the back of the cemetery. She's staring off into the distance, and her image is translucent and semitransparent.

With care, I step and slide down the dew-covered incline to where she sits. I duck behind a small elm a few yards from her. From my position, I can watch her as I gather my nerve.

She appears so tiny and vulnerable. I can't help but wonder what she thinks as she sits on the stone surface as the world goes on without her. Who is she waiting for?

The voices in the cemetery claw at the wall I built in my mind. I need to act soon. If I stay close to so many dead much longer, I won't be able to keep them out.

As I step from behind the tree, we lock eyes and she shimmers brighter. Her head tilts to the right, and she appears to try and place me.

"I've seen you before." Her voice is so lucid it startles me.

"The casino," I croak. "You saw me in the coffee shop."

She nearly smiles before her face twitches into a snarl. "Brodie threw me out again tonight. He told me to go home to my mama."

The familiarity shocks me. "You know the security guard?"

"Sure, I do. I went to school with his son Elijah."

As I approach the stone monument, I read the name inscribed *Alexandria Sharpton*. The engraving records her death as 1903. "What's your name?"

"Memory Reid. My mama always said it would be easy for folks to remember."

I laugh. "I'm pleased to meet you, Memory Reid. I'm April May Snow."

She narrows her eyes in disbelief. "Are you for real, or are you pulling my leg?"

"My parents have a sense of humor, too."

Memory crosses her arms. "And I thought I had it bad."

We grin at each other, but our expressions turn somber as the awkward silence fills the air. Memory begins to dim as she turns her head, returning her stare toward the casino. The longing in her demeanor cuts at my heart.

I don't want to give you the false impression I know what I'm doing regarding spiritual beings. Yes, I've seen ghosts regularly since I was eight. And since the age of twelve, I've heard their voices.

But still, they are a mystery to me. Each entity is profoundly different and complicated.

Mostly, I try to avoid them when I can or pretend not to see them. Some, like Alvin, can tell immediately I can communicate with the dead. Fortunately, others aren't as astute.

Something about Memory Reid makes me want to help. I'm not sure if it's because she's close to my age or the lost expression on her face. But I know I want to help her if I have the ability.

The longer we are silent, the more she dims. If I don't engage her soon, she'll disappear for the night. I swallow hard and ask, "Memory, not to be insensitive, but you know you're…"

"Dead? Yeah, it took me a few years, but I figured it out."

"So, if you know you're dead, are you here by choice?"

She brightens, and her face pinches in. "Are you kidding me? Why would I want to remain here in someone else's crypt?"

"I meant this plane."

"No, my mama." She frowns back to the casino and pauses. I

assume she will say nothing else in explanation.

Her head snaps back around, and her eyes lock with mine. "By the time I figured out I was dead, she moved. I kept hoping she might visit the casino and I could let her know. I'm sure she's still worried about me."

Her staying behind makes sense to me in some odd mama-daughter relationship matrix. I know if I came up missing and my body wasn't found, I would hang back and try to send word to my mama. I would want her to start the healing process, and I don't believe she could until she knew what happened to me.

"Do you have any other ideas where she might be? I mean, besides hoping she might come into the casino?"

She shakes her head, and I see a silver tear streak down her cheek.

"Friends? Family?"

"It was only the two of us. We moved around a lot." She clutches her hands in her lap. "I've tried every place I can think of to find her."

I know it isn't what she's asking or concerned about, but I can't help but ask. "Memory, were you killed?"

She shrugs. "I've no clue. I was walking home, and the next thing I knew, I was walking through town and no one could see me. At first, I didn't think much about it. Given most people in this town know what my job is, it's not unusual for them to act like I'm invisible to them. But eventually, I figured it out."

"You don't remember anything? No details to help the police determine what happened to you?"

Memory's color darkens, and she appears agitated. "You don't get it. It doesn't matter. What does matter is I don't want my mama thinking I'm going to walk through her front door someday."

Fair. And if her mama being aware she is dead is all Memory needs to be at peace. I figure if her mother is still alive, it'll be easy for me to help her.

Memory continues to stare in the direction of the casino. Slowly her form pixelates until she has the appearance of a silver holograph.

I watch in silence, and I formulate a plan in my mind. As the inky, dark sky turns navy blue, she folds in onto herself, forming the silver-mist orb again.

I'm not surprised the orb sinks into the top of the sarcophagus, like a sunset into the Pacific. Memory complained about being in someone else's crypt. The orb only confirmed the suspicion that crystallized in my mind.

Stepping forward, I press the palms of my hands against the rough stone cover and push with all my might. The lid rotates four inches, leaving a small crack open below my hands. The stench of fetid flesh and cinnamon assaults my nose.

I turn my head from the smell and feel sweat trickle from my forehead. I rub my brow on my sleeve. *You can do this, April.*

Gritting my teeth, I suck in my gut and slam my palms on the cover. This time the lid swivels with some momentum, and I follow it around the front of the grave, lunging forward wildly. The stone slab stops at the edge of the sarcophagus. It teeters up, and as I think the lid will crash to the earth, it settles cattywampus on the base.

The effort sapped the last of my energy, leaving me winded and nearly too tired to inspect the grave.

But in for a penny, in for a pound. Besides, after desecrating a grave, I might as well satisfy my voracious curiosity and see if my hunch is correct.

I peer into the sarcophagus and jump back at the shadowed skull I see. Really? What was I expecting?

I shine my flashlight in and give it another attempt. The skull is detached and lying to the left of the shrouded body. Odd.

I thought by the twentieth century, people had already dropped the custom of burying in shrouds and begun dressing the dead in their clothes. Yet the occupant is wrapped in cloth.

Something isn't quite right. The shrouded body still has a head, plus there's a detached skull next to the shroud. Any way you count it, there's an extra head in the grave.

I reach for the shroud, and my gag reflex kicks in before I touch the dusty, yellow fabric. Let me tell you, I've seen some seriously messed up things in my life. Apparitions most people would call nightmares, but those experiences don't make uncovering a real dead body any easier. Dead bodies, especially ones in the later stages of decay, have smells that are extreme yuck and make my skin crawl. I can numb myself to sights, but smell is such a primal sense my body reacts on autopilot, and they are impossible for me to ignore.

The shroud won't come undone. I pull on the hem again, and it holds tight around what I believe is the body's neck.

I notice a chalky band of duct tape. It's deteriorated into one fibrous length of sticky glue. I curse myself for not having my pocketknife with me. I can visualize all the men in my family saying in unison, "See, you never know when you'll need it."

My apartment key will have to do in a pinch. I run my key back and forth across the goo. Fortunately, I will only be in my apartment for a few more weeks because this key will be garbage after this impromptu use as a cutting tool.

The tape finally gives up the ghost, and I'm nearly spent. I muster one last burst of strength to pull on the shroud. A portion unravels.

I squint at the jumble of clues revealed at once.

First, I'm not pulling on a burial shroud. It's a deteriorating bed sheet. Second, I might as well save my energy since there is more duct tape to cut through further down the body. There appears to be more tape around what I assume to be the waist and knees of the corpse.

Last and most horrifying, there is definitely an extra head in the grave. One skull is white ivory and the second skull from inside the sheet stares out with black, putrefied eyeballs. A few scraps of deteriorating flesh cling to the forehead and petrified ears of the second skull.

Is this Memory? I wish I could be sure.

I feel it must be her. It would explain why her spirit lingers at a grave with someone else's name.

I can't be sure. It will require a forensic team days to sort this dilemma out and identify the two people sharing this grave. So much for the easy slam dunk of letting Memory's mama know what has happened to her daughter.

Now I need to figure out how to close the lid back onto the sarcophagus without letting it accidentally fall on me and crush my legs. That's going to be fun on this hot and humid night.

I take a position to push the lid, keeping my feet strategically well behind me in case the cover slides off the base.

Something below the duct tape around the body's knees catches my eye. I'm not sure how I missed it earlier. I reach in and lift the petite, red platform shoe—gray with caked dust from the sarcophagus—and hold it to my chest.

This is Memory. I don't need a DNA test to prove my theory. As I suspected, someone stashed her body in this old sarcophagus. Her murderer correctly assumed no search party would violate graves when they canvassed the grid decades ago in search of her.

Now I need to get Memory home and let her mama know her little girl is no longer missing. Assuming her mama is still alive.

I place the dusty, red shoe back into the sarcophagus. I consider whether I should try to slide the lid back into place. Instead, I surmise there is as much chance of me knocking it to the ground as being able to push it closed. Besides, I'll be placing the phone call to the authorities in the next hour. With any luck, Memory will be with the medical examiner by morning.

"Someone will be coming for you soon, Memory." I pull the brittle, yellowed sheet up to cover her decayed face. It just seems like the proper thing to do.

When I pull up, a tarnished hoop rolls toward the back of the sarcophagus. I grab at the muted gold band, and I go blind.

Chapter 13

My ankle twists as my ridiculously high platform shoes roll to the side. The pain in my shoulder and elbow intensify.

"Walk," a man growls in my ear.

Regaining my footing eases the pressure of my arm pinned behind my back. I recognize the Delta Queen casino lobby, but everything is wrong. The slots look different, the backing behind the check-in area is a different color, and the snack bar is missing.

Too busy looking, I trip again as we exit through the glass doors onto the pavement. The man lifts me by my arm again.

"I've had it with your shenanigans, Memory. I have warned you for the last time. You take your business elsewhere or I'll fix it where you don't have to worry about—"

He stops short. Still, I feel his hostility burning against my back. "You're hurting me."

"You're lucky I'm not hurting you. But this is it. The next time you show up here, I promise you it will be your last."

The warm, moist air and the pain in my arm has beads of sweat popping up on my skin. I have to focus on my steps as the man's shoves cause me to wobble on my platform shoes.

The man stops shoving me momentarily as a Saturn S-series in mint condition drives in front of us with its windows down. The voices of George Michael and Elton John pour out the window, singing, "Don't Let the Sun Go Down On Me." I look up and notice the plethora of new Ford Taurus cars and Chrysler minivans in the parking lot.

"You say a word, and I swear it will be your last."

I catch my breath as I understand my predicament. "Brodie?"

"I said shut your mouth," he growls.

The Saturn pulls into a parking space. Brodie pushes me forward.

Is this it? Is Brodie the one who killed Memory and hid her in the grave of Alexandria Sharpton.

"Where are you taking me?"

"Since you can't follow directions, I figured I'd make sure to escort you off the property."

"You don't have to do this." I can't tell if the thoughts are mine or Memory's. Everything is a jumble in my head.

"Yes—I—do! It's my job."

We reach the edge of the property, and my anxiety peaks. It's not that I believe I can prevent Memory's murder, because I can't. Still, I don't care to relive it from her point of view.

I turn around quickly, bringing my left hand around, catching Brodie on his left ear. He releases my arm, which is my hope.

Stepping back away from him as he recovers, he lunges for me. He grabs at my shoulder, and the palms of his hands slam into my clavicle.

I teeter backward on my platform heels for what feels like an eternity. Reaching out toward Brodie, he makes to grab my wrists as his eyes open wide. His hand bumps my wrist, and his nails scratch me as he misses my arm.

My heel slides back a fraction of an inch. Catching the lip of the curb, I lean back at an improbable angle. I see the full moon above me, close my eyes, and wait for the impact as I fall backward.

Chapter 14

I sit up from the dew-covered grass. Leaning forward, I put my hand to my forehead to gather my thoughts.

As I rest at the base of her sarcophagus, the voices of other earthbound spirits in the cemetery increase in volume to a crescendo. I'm forced to squint my eyes as I try to keep a migraine at bay. The residents felt my foray into Memory's past. They understand I will assist Memory to come to peace, and they want the same help.

I can't concentrate. The building pressure in my head makes me dizzy.

Turning over onto all fours, I consider the chore of standing and returning to the casino. It seems so far, and the thought of the task is overwhelming. A profound, general sadness covers my spirit, and my mind is filled with despair.

My mental partitions crash down like the walls of Jericho. I feel it, and I understand it has happened. I also know how dangerous that development is for me while I am near so many dead.

With great labor, I force myself to stand. I stumble up the hill toward the oak tree, twisting my ankle on the unlevel footing more than once.

My stomach roils as I reach the tree, and my dinner fights its way up. I hold it at bay—barely—and lean forward, head between my legs and my hand on the tree bark. I take a few deep breaths, steadying my stomach, and I glance up to see how much further I have to travel to the cemetery gate.

I attempt to ignore the multitudes of loosely formed apparitions dotting the cemetery grounds now. Still, I can't ignore their pleas. Again, I try to strengthen the mental barrier which normally mutes their voices, but it's an act of futility.

Fine. It can't be more than a hundred yards to the gate, despite the exit having rotated into a different direction again. I better get busy before the graveyard plays ring around the twisted, scary oak tree again. I'll focus on putting one foot in front of the other and speed walk my way out.

The tree bark moves under my hand, and I drop to one knee as I jerk my hand back. I reach back out with my hand to catch myself before my face crashes into the tree trunk.

The faces outlined in the bark I saw earlier begin to move. Their lips curl into ferocious snarls as a few grow fangs protruding like spears from the tree.

I do a double-take and freeze. I'm simultaneously horrified and mesmerized by the caricatures' eyes blinking and lips moving on the bark as a light buzzing sound emanates from the tree.

It's as if the tree is whispering but too quiet to be intelligible. I lean closer to their whispering lips despite their ghastly expressions.

"Nourish the acorn, blood of the witch on the soil, bring forth the forest."

I frown as I pull back from the buzzing voices. A haiku? Now, if that isn't just—

"Fudge biscuit." I pull my hand from the tree, gritting my teeth and clenching my fist.

The hairs on my arms stand on end as I watch droplets of blood fall to the earth. A shiver works its way up my spine.

I look back at the tree, and the faces now grin. One that resembles a hawkish-featured man licks his wooden lips with a tongue that appeared as quickly as the multiple bloodied fangs protruding from where my hand had been.

I'm still staring in horror at the diabolical tree as my feet run for the front gate.

I turn my head in time to hurdle a tombstone. I land on the next grave's stone marker, and the earth gives under my weight. The spongy, unnatural texture makes me think of a massive marshmallow. My knees buckle as I try to step out of the grave. I claw at the edge of the indention to scramble to freedom.

"Why don't you sit a spell, dear." A grandmotherly figure sits on the tombstone to my left, sipping silver liquid from a glass.

"I don't belong here!" I whip my head in the direction of the scream of despair. A blue-and-silver cloud swirls toward me from the far side of the cemetery. The cloud takes on the loose formation of a young woman's face—sans body.

My sandals clear the mush earth of the grave I landed in, and I tear up ground toward the gate. Focusing on my escape, I pretend not to notice the multiple swirls of blue, silver, and pitch-black clouds that begin to leak from the multitude of graves.

Twenty yards from the gate, the cemetery shifts. The inertia makes me fall to the ground, and as I look up, I see the gate now on the west side of the cemetery.

I run the two hundred yards to the gate at top speed, praying that the spin is some random timing and has nothing to do with my proximity to the entrance.

My shin clips a tombstone, nearly causing me to crash to the ground again. Instead, I fight for my balance and am back up to full speed in two steps.

Who knew I could run this fast?

I slam my right palm onto the center of the gate. The impact vibrates up my elbow. Geez, that'll smart later, but I have more significant issues following me right now.

I open the gate in one smooth motion, then spin to sling it shut before tearing down the cracked concrete sidewalk toward the casino. Stopping isn't an option, but I gasp for air a few yards after fleeing the cemetery. I'm afraid I'll suck every bug in Mississippi out of the sky if I don't take a break.

I don't have a choice. I stop to rest, doubling over with my hands on my knees. My body is leaking sweat.

The other spirits in the cemetery remind me why I avoid any place people have died or been buried. It's just too much.

Don't get me wrong. I would help all of them if I could.

Still, the longer spirits stay on this side of the veil when they should have moved on, the crazier they get. If I try to help them, most won't be able to tell me what I need to do to give them peace. Then there's a considerable number of spirits staying on this side of the veil because they know what they have earned during their lives. They're hoping for some celestial appeal process that will never happen.

Memory is different. She's still aware enough to recognize I can see her. And, though her behavior at this point has almost become a loop, she has a set purpose. She's hoping her mother visits the casino and she can contact her.

The further I walk from the cemetery, the more pleased I become I'm going to help her. That I can help.

No, it's not on the same level of accomplishment as defending someone wrongfully accused of a crime or helping someone reach a goal they thought couldn't be achieved. But I'm going to help Memory. I'm going to help her bring peace and closure to her mother.

Never mind the fact she's a ghost. She's still human.

I first need to contact the authorities, but I can't use my phone since I want to remain anonymous. I saw a bank of pay phones in the hotel lobby, artifacts from a day gone by. With any luck, they are still in working condition. If I use those phones, the authorities can trace me to the Delta Queen, but there are many guests staying there.

The night feels much colder now that I am walking rather than running. My spirit lightens with each step closer to the casino.

I'll simply make an anonymous call to the police, letting them know where they can find the body of Memory Reid. Next, I'll go upstairs and catch a nap. Easy peasy.

What about Brodie?

That's a tough one. He did, albeit inadvertently, kill Memory.

I'm torn. On the one hand, I agree with Memory. What matters is making sure her mother can move on with her life.

Still, Brodie disposed of Memory as if she were a piece of garbage. Not a human being. I can't get okay with that. It irks.

I suppose it's good that I have not seen Brodie around on the grounds. If he were, I would certainly figure out a way to tie him to Memory's death.

I'll ask around. Find out what I can about Brodie and his whereabouts, just in case I can't honor Memory's request to let that part lie.

I go to pull my phone from my back pocket and realize I have something balled up in my left fist. My chest tightens as I look at the tarnished gold hoop in my hand.

Chapter 15

The phone call to the authorities in the morning is anticlimactic. The dispatcher asks me several questions I decline to answer. I know to keep to the facts. Memory Reid's body shares the sarcophagus with Alexandria Sharpton in the old town cemetery.

No, I won't tell you my name. No, I don't know how she got there. And no, I don't know who killed her. Click.

I wanted to say it was Brodie. But it seemed sort of stupid since I don't even know his last name or if he is alive.

Concise is better anyway. It's best to hang up when a call isn't going the way you want it to. Besides, I already made my point. They will send someone to check the cemetery even if they think I'm a prank caller.

I walk out the back door of the Delta Queen. The Olympic-size pool is quiet now except for the muted mechanical hum of the filtration system. The smell of chlorine hangs thick, mingling with the scent of vegetation decay blowing on the wind from the west.

Opening the gate, I walk onto the greenway and raise my eyes to the horizon. The navy blue is beginning to lighten to lavender, and the moon has eased to the western sky.

A new day will be here soon.

Memory will be free to travel to the other side soon, too.

It's not the same. Fundamentally I know this, but there are some similarities between Memory's and my own situation. Well, nobody killed me, but we're both waiting "until."

Memory is waiting until she knows her mother is notified of her death. I'm waiting for Jan to let me know I can come to work and draw a paycheck.

I know they are not comparable. But I'm feeling sorry for myself as the last of the adrenaline drains away, and I guess I'm getting a little melodramatic.

It's just I'm not used to this "hanging in limbo" thing. It doesn't suit me. I'm a creature of making and executing plans. Not biding my time and waiting my turn.

But here I am in my own version of purgatory, waiting to cross over to the other side. I can't wait to cross over to the gainfully employed side of life.

The lavender sky transforms into a brilliant lilac before shifting to a salmon color. In the presence of true beauty, it's hard to stay aggravated.

I take a seat on the beach and push my toes deep into the cool sand. I feel the last of the stress dissipate from my body.

Watching the slow transformation of the sky calms my breathing. Things are shifting back into relevance, and I remember how small I am and how limited my days are in the more enormous scope of things.

I'm glad nobody else is on the beach yet as I laugh aloud like a crazy person. I can't believe I let those lovebirds talk me into driving them down here. What in the world was I thinking?

Lord, I've done some spur-of-the-moment things before, but this is plum near stupid. But, oddly, everything might work out for all of us in the end. I'm not just talking about financially, either. I have a feeling Trent, Sonia, and I will be forever linked into a loose friendship for the rest of our lives from the shared experience of this crazy trip.

One thing I know, you can't have enough friends. Even if they are a little touched.

Chapter 16

I stay on the beach longer than I intend, watching the gulls and sandpipers scour the beach for their breakfast. The quiet time does me well. I don't believe I fully understood how much the stress of my financial situation and the recent increase in the regularity of ghost sightings weighs on my energy level.

Reluctantly, I stand and wipe the sand off my butt and thighs. If the sun weren't already baking the skin on the back of my neck, I would curl up and sleep in the fresh breeze for a few days.

Guests are already bringing bagels, cereal, and reconstituted scrambled eggs out onto the deck, signaling it's after six since the breakfast bar is open. Hopefully, Sonia and Trent are still asleep.

I develop a pang of guilt. I hope they didn't worry about me last night.

While waiting for the elevator, I scold myself. It would've been ten times easier to send Sonia a text message telling her I'd be late rather than explain this morning.

I enter our motel room. Trent and Sonia have dressed and are collecting their belongings. "Good morning." I hope to skate through the situation by making it sound reasonable that I didn't sleep in our room last night.

"There you are. Is everything alright?" Sonia asks as she picks up her purse.

"Yes, I was having a terrible time sleeping, so I went for a walk."

The dam of guilt breaks. "I'm sorry I didn't text you last night and let you know where I was. I had a lot on my mind, and I didn't think about it."

"Don't worry about it. I got concerned when we woke up, but Trent went downstairs looking for you and said he found you on the beach."

I must appear as shocked as I feel. Trent's eyes lock with mine, and he blushes. "You were miles away in thought, so I wanted to let you have your time alone."

"Yeah, I suppose there's been a lot on my mind lately."

"But a lot less to worry about after your winnings yesterday," Sonia interjects. "You've got all the money you need, and in a few hours, Trent and I will be set, too."

An uneasy feeling rises in my gut again. A burning urge consumes me, driving my desire to try again to explain why we should leave right now. Seeing my new friends in front of me this morning only makes it more urgent. Even if it means Trent must give up his five-thousand-dollar entry fee, I believe it would be money well lost.

I can't explain the desperate urge. Call it the third rail of understanding, but I feel a growing anxiety that money will be the least of our issues if we stay and play games today.

I open my mouth to object but shut it instead. The expressions of excitement and expectation on their faces make me remain silent. If I can't explain my unease to myself, how am I supposed to explain the premonitions to my friends?

"Are you going to join us for breakfast, April?" Trent asks.

Oddly, after the considerable walking and physical exertion of last night, I'm still not the least bit hungry. What I am is exhausted. "I hope y'all don't mind, but I'd like to stay in the room and sleep until you're ready to go home."

"Are you sure?" Sonia asks.

"I'm positive. You two go enjoy yourself as a couple without a third wheel today, and win the grand prize. I'm gonna stay up here and rest up so I can drive us all home safely."

"Would you like me to bring you something up?" Trent asks.

I gesture for them to leave the room. "The biggest favor you can give me right now is to let me sleep. I think my mind is finally clear enough to catch some Z's."

"Okay. If you're sure."

I put my hand on Trent's shoulder and push him gently toward the door. "I promise I'll call if I change my mind."

I crash onto the pull-out bed as the hotel door closes. My shorts and shirt must come off for the hibernation nap I plan, and I need to wash my face and brush my teeth. Still, all those tasks sound like they require a lot of effort.

Instead, I curl into a fetal position as I hug one of my pillows. It is a struggle to ignore the day-old makeup on my face as I consider if I'll be blessed with a field of blemishes when I wake.

As the first fogginess of sleep comes over me, my mind drifts to Memory Reid. I wonder if the police have found her yet and if they've removed her from the sarcophagus.

It's a tragedy what happened to Memory. It's a nightmare I assume parents secretly harbor each time their children leave the house. The horror that their baby might come up missing, and they'll never be able to ask them about their day, tell them they love them, or give them a hug again.

Despite the horror of what was, I have a warm, soft glow in my chest from having been able to help Memory and her mama find peace.

I don't know the rules and regulations of this spirit communication game. But I feel like I muddled through the situation with Memory much like I did in the case of Rhonda Riley at my sorority house. Both times I believe I did all right. At least I let their spirits move closer to the next plane of existence.

Having a skill and no finite directions about how it works really bites. In the end, I do the best I can with the scant information available to me.

The dream from yesterday flashes across my consciousness, and I become anxious about falling asleep. I don't care to get the second version of the confusing images. But with the happy feelings from my good deed, I ignore my apprehensions and give over to sleep.

I wonder what the first responders thought when they peered into the sarcophagus. They had to give a double take when they found two skulls in the same grave.

It was a darn near perfect place to hide a murder victim, whoever the killer was. It's not likely anyone would've ever found Memory since she was in someone else's grave.

My deep sleep transforms over to a now-familiar vision. I walk on the casino's geometrically designed carpet floor, and the pit boss follows me. I watch his reflection a few feet behind in the mirrored black partition as I move from one aisle of slot machines to the next. There's a comfortable distance between us, and I feel I could lose him conveniently if I wanted to.

I turn to my left. Six feet in front of me, the hallway ends. I've nowhere to go, and I'm trapped. I wait for the pit boss, but he never comes. Then multiple cracking noises reverberate down the hall.

I sit straight up in bed. Man, I don't know what Leon put in that cupcake he gave me, but I think it's got me tripping.

So much for a long nap. There's no chance I'm going to fall back to sleep now.

Flipping on the TV, I hope to accomplish two things. First, distract me from the recurring dream giving me the heebie-jeebies. Second, hopefully, I will find some information about Memory. I don't want to be left guessing if she's been found.

I can't find a news channel since it's a little after nine. I give up and stare blankly at the start of a game show I remember watching as a child. It horrifies me how badly the host and hostess have aged.

A red-and-yellow banner scrolls along the bottom of the TV screen as the words "Breaking News" appear. I lean toward the television as more words trail across the screen.

Memory Reid, a local nursing student, missing since the fall of 1998, has been found. Police were led to her body by an anonymous tip...Police have no comment on current suspects... Miss Reid is survived by her mother, Tanya Reid, who has been notified of her daughter's death.

There it is. The report I've been waiting for. I only wish I could have been with Memory's mama to comfort her when she received the heart-wrenching news. Having your suspicions confirmed that your only daughter is never coming home must be devastating. Her misery would be compounded by the fact Tanya has no one else to lean on.

Hopefully, she'll make it through this ordeal. I believe knowing must be better than still being in a constant holding pattern while waiting for information.

Interestingly, the police took the time to make a statement regarding no current suspects. I wonder if they ever much thought of Memory Reid over the last twenty years. They might have already had suspects and found her body without my help if they did.

The important thing is she's home now, and I did everything in my power to improve the situation. Everything else is out of my control.

Happy that I know my call to the authorities had the desired outcome, and knowing I will never fall back to sleep, I take a shower.

As I dry my hair, my stomach growls, announcing I'm hungrier than I thought. Between the hunger and the boredom, I decide to call Sonia and find out how they're faring.

"Hey." Sonia's voice is barely a whisper.

"Did I catch you at a bad time?"

"No. Trent made it into the quarterfinal, and they're down to four tables now."

I sit up straight and smile. "Well, there's some exciting news."

"I know, right?"

"Well, I hope he wins all the money in this joint. That'll guarantee we eat like royalty tonight."

"You're awful."

"I prefer to call it pragmatic. I was about to go down to the café and get myself a sandwich. Do you guys need anything?"

"No. We snacked right before Trent took his seat. But thank you for asking."

"All right. Best of luck. I'll see you in a little while."

I can't help but laugh at our good fortune as I hang up the phone. How perfect will it be if we leave Biloxi with the money we hoped to win on this loony trip? Of course, no one will ever believe us.

I pick up my purse and phone and head to the café. It looks like I'm going to be eating alone. Assuming no ghost decides to crash my solitude.

I learned my lesson the other morning. I order *one* of those fancy omelets the chef cooks and a single spoonful of fried potatoes. The last thing I want is a bloated gut when we finally make good on our escape from Biloxi.

Sadly, I'm nervous about the end of our adventure because of my recurring dream and how it causes my skin to prickle as if a thousand ants are crawling on me. If it weren't for the troubling vision, I'd be relaxing by the pool or playing the slots to pass the time today.

But I find it impossible to relax when I feel like there's another shoe left to drop. A heavy, steel-toed one, too.

My omelet is incredible. It's almost worth the fifteen dollars I paid. I was unaware the meal tabs Trent and Sonia were covering were this expensive.

Oddly, as much as I like free, it is liberating to pay my way this morning. Having money in my pocket does a lot for improving my attitude.

One of the large-screen TVs breaks away from the less-than-scintillating broadcast of a bunch of dudes playing golf. My fork hovers inches from my mouth. A woman who resembles an age progression version of Memory appears on the screen. The woman seems to be in her early- to mid-seventies or, more likely, a rode hard and put up wet sixty-year-old.

An identifying banner, in white, appears below her weeping vision. It isn't necessary. I already know it's Tanya Reid.

I wish I could hear what she's saying. She's at a podium flanked by a stout man in a three-piece suit and a sharp-dressed police official.

My eyes tear up as I watch her. Part empathy for a mother living through a tragic situation and part happiness she hopefully, with time, can heal. I'm glad I could help bring her peace.

Tanya's tears continue to stream, and she dabs at them with a tissue as she speaks. Between the many lifts of her hand to her eyes, I lip-read the words "my baby" and "thank you" several times.

Wow. What sort of woman can gather so much gratitude and strength to express appreciation when her world has been destroyed? Then I remember the scrappy nature of her daughter's apparition, and I smile. Daughters are more like their mothers than we ever like to admit.

The portly official in the three-piece suit helps Ms. Reid off camera. When the distinguished-looking police official steps forward, the TV station switches coverage back to the golf tournament. I'm sure it's much more important to know if the short dude in yellow pants makes the birdie shot on thirteen than if the police have any suspects in Memory's murder case.

I draw in a deep breath and release it slowly. In the scheme of things, it doesn't matter if the police have a suspect. Whether they do or don't and whether anyone is held responsible for the crime or not, Memory is still gone, and her mama will always be alone. Some things can't be fixed.

I slide my hand into my pocket and pull out the badly tarnished hoop earring I accidentally lifted from her grave. I dip my cloth napkin into my water and attempt to wipe the tarnish off with little success.

It's odd. I fancy I can feel the slightest tingle resonating from Memory's earring.

Of course, that's just nonsense. It's me regretting what happened to her and feeling connected to her somehow.

I never knew her. Yet, I know exactly who she was. A survivor, a woman who made no excuses for doing what she felt she needed to do to advance to a better life. Brodie just killed her before she could make her career change.

Man, I need something to get my mind off this.

I drop a five on the table for the bus waiter and stretch my hands over my head as I steal a glance in the direction of the game room entry. Oh, how the golden arch of the game floor is calling me. Not with the same strength and intensity as a cupcake or a new pair of shoes, but I feel the itch.

Hey, if I'm honest with myself, it's way too hot to lay out by the pool. I don't want to take another shower to wash the chlorine off me anyway. Plus, sitting in my room and watching soap operas would drive me nuts.

I'm in a casino. What will it hurt to play for a couple of hours while Trent wins the regional poker tourney if I'm responsible?

Yep, my mind's made up, and I nonchalantly stroll toward the entry of sin and obsession. Granny would be so ashamed of me.

Chapter 17

Approaching the game floor, I can't help but pan my view side to side, searching for paranormal entities. My internal ghost meter is twitching in the red, but I don't see anything today.

Perfect. If the dead keep to themselves, I'll keep to myself.

I sit down at the first slot machine, only six feet onto the diametric carpet. It's like dipping my foot into the pool. All I need to do is stand up and take three steps to exit the casino area. Surely, I have the discipline to take three steps if I believe I am losing control.

A twenty-dollar bill seems like a safe, responsible bet. When the twenty-dollar tally shows up on the screen, I give over to the restless craving and settle onto my backless stool. Oh yeah. I'm going to win so many coins I will need a wheel barrel to roll them over to the cashiers.

My twenty dollars dissipates so fast my seat cushion hasn't warmed to the temperature of my butt yet. I guess they don't call them one-armed bandits for nothing. What a scam.

I push off the stool and consider my options. The responsible and cautious April's internal voice recommends that I take three steps out of the casino to see what other diversions can occupy my time. The addictive personality April reminds me I am a champ at the blackjack tables.

I head deeper into the casino lair.

Yes, this feels better. I sigh in relief as I spy a table with an open lead chair to my left. My lucky position at the table. I barely settle onto the soft top of my high-backed bar stool before I feel a tap on my shoulder.

I turn my head and nearly pee myself in shock. I'm looking into the hard-set dark eyes of the pit boss.

"You need to come with me."

"I don't think so." It isn't the best answer, but it rolls out of my mouth before I can think.

"Miss, I'm only going to ask you politely one more time."

Geez. I was only looking to kill a couple hours and possibly make a few bucks. The last thing I want to do is escalate this until I'm being strip-searched by the pit boss or whatever else they do in their back room.

I collect my purse and step off the stool with a dramatic huff. The pit boss gestures with his hand, and I follow him over to an area free of other patrons.

"What's this about?" I can't hold my water any longer.

He turns toward me and glowers at me. His expression practically dares me to lie to him. "You're counting cards."

My face flutters in and out of about five different expressions at once. I am the world's worst liar, and I know the only way I will get out of this is to tell a big fat one. "I haven't played today."

"We're not talking about today, are we?"

"I assumed we were."

"You got lucky yesterday. If I had gotten to you before you left the table, I would've taken back the house's money."

So, Alvin was right. If I ever see him again, I'll need to thank him again. I start to reply to Pit Boss and decide it's best to stay quiet and see how this plays out.

His eyes squint as he leans closer to me. "I know your type. You think you can come down here and take advantage of the locals. Mind you, I've had years of experience in this job, and I've brushed back the best of them."

Pit Boss is so close to me that his energy overlaps mine, and I sense something dreadful that explains the odd smell on his breath.

My heart sinks, and another log of anxiety and angst is thrown onto the ever-growing bonfire of concern raging in my mind. While trying to hold a calm face on the outside, I am screaming one word in my mind. *No!*

Never before have I had such a detailed reading of someone without touching them. I might get an aggravating tingle when I am near an evil person, similar to the sensation I have when a spirit is close. Still, nothing like the information dump I am receiving off Pit Boss's aura.

This is a disaster. It can only mean my "gifts" are increasing in strength again. The opposite of what I want.

Fantastic. As if I don't already have enough oddity to hide from the world.

As I stare into the dark eyes of Pit Boss and try not to grimace at the noxious sickly energy emanating from him, I realize it's best to stay silent.

Unfortunately, I tend to talk more than I should when stressed. The first thing that comes to my mind slips out of my mouth. "I know it's none of my business, but the pain you've been feeling in your stomach, you need to get it checked out today."

Pit Boss's eyes open in shock. "My stomach? How did you? You can't know that."

I try to keep a straight face as I uncork a doozy. "I'm a physician's assistant. I'm trained in all manners of diagnoses of advanced diseases. Your breath has a specific smell, indicating you have a 97.3 percent chance of having stage four stomach cancer. Take an expert's word. You don't have much time to treat it if you don't want to die."

Pit Boss takes a faltering step back and examines me like I'm an alien. He opens his mouth to say something else, closes it as he shakes his head, and pivots away from me.

I frown as I watch him speed walk off toward the exit of the casino gaming room.

Gross. I don't want to be able to pick up on people's illnesses. Besides leaving a nasty after scent in my nasal cavity, that gift would be totally wasted on me. If I had known I had that in my whacky bag of gifts, I would have become a doctor. It's sort of a lost talent when an attorney has that skill.

I hope I only sensed his terminal illness because of the extreme nature of the situation. Not everyone will be three inches from my face and be only a few weeks away from death in a highly stressful situation.

Hopefully, I'm wrong—about the terminal illness part—and the doctors can do something for Pit Boss. Even if he is a jerk.

I walk back in the direction of the blackjack game Pit Boss pulled me from but notice the camera prominently over the table. The probability is he has a couple of partners to take his place. If I play anything, it will have to be the slot machines or something that doesn't involve cards.

Wait. What about the craps table? I can't be accused of counting dice. Right?

Chapter 18

Excitement is practically bubbling out of me as I make my way to the craps table. I'm trying to remember what Chase told me about the game. He said something about only playing the pass out line and the don't pass out line? No, that's not right.

Dang, why didn't I pay attention when he was explaining?

Easy. It was Chase, and he was telling me something I wasn't interested in at the time. If I paid attention to him all the time, I'd be able to rebuild a 350 short block and win the next bass tournament on Guntersville Lake.

I have zero interest in doing either.

A familiar face comes into my view at the first craps table. Alvin groans at the results of the current dice roll. Throwing his luminescent hands into the air, he hollers, "You gotta be kidding me!" He yanks at his blond spiked hair. Our eyes meet, and his frown becomes a lopsided grin.

"Don't tell me my favorite girl is going to try a real game today."

I begin to answer him before I remember I am the only person in the room who can see him. I improvise with a language I know Alvin understands and favor him a thumbs up.

Alvin pumps the air with his fist as he moves to my side of the table. "Awesome choice. You won't be disappointed. Let me give you a few pointers first, though. Because the table will be confusing if you've never played."

I move between two older men at the table as Alvin gestures me forward.

"Now, until you get your bearings in the game, I want you to play the pass and don't pass line. It will allow you to get your feet wet without losing your cash too quickly."

It's idiotic, but a laugh bubbles up from inside me. First, pass line versus passed out makes a lot more sense. Second, Alvin said the exact same thing as my brother Chase. It must be a guy thing.

Alvin tilts his head to the right. "What's so funny?"

"Nothing. I'm excited, is all," I mumble as if I am talking to myself.

A wild expression spreads across Alvin's face. "You should be. This is the most exciting game in the entire casino." He rubs his hands together. "Are you ready to place your first bet?"

Without hesitation, I pull a hundred-dollar bill out of my purse. I know the addiction is growing, but it will only be for today.

"I like it. I love a woman with confidence."

I ignore Alvin as I give the stick man my hundred and exchange it for chips. I place a single chip on the pass line as Alvin instructed. A lady sitting to my right rolls the dice, and an eleven comes up.

"You win," Alvin informs me.

Well, this is easier than blackjack. I like this game.

I lean against the thick wooden lip of the table. My interest was piqued by the easy win. The colors and numbers of the tables seem brighter as my mind is fully engaged on how to crush this new game.

The dealer puts a matching chip on top of my original bet. I notice the dice pass from one woman to the next player.

"So, what they're doing is called the pass. On a seven or eleven, the players pass the dice. Two, three, or twelve is craps, and anything else establishes the number."

"The number?" I mumble.

A man across the table looks up and squints at me, trying to discern if I was asking a question to the group. I favor him with a quick smile, and he looks back to the table.

"Yes, number." Alvin studies the blank look on my face. His enthusiasm cools. "Never mind. Let's keep it simple for now and continue to play the pass line."

The game is easy until it isn't. When we establish a number, a term meaning nothing to me, the game becomes more complicated.

Still, Alvin is a patient mentor. I guess if you're dead, it might be a little easier to display patience.

Curious, I try my psychic abilities on the dice roll. I know it's not wise to risk strengthening my "gifts," *but if I can...*

Besides, this is an entirely different scale than playing blackjack. My heart beats so fast that I can barely catch my breath. This is where I was meant to be all along.

The whole point of this cockamamie trip was to win money. Specifically, a hundred grand. I'd be a ghost by the time I won that amount playing blackjack, and especially with security watching me like a hawk.

No, if I am to believe in the whole manifestation idea, this feels like the right place since there are hundreds of chips on the table begging for me to win them. So, keeping with the plan, I should be able to bring my other "gifts" to bear on this manifestation project. Right?

To my surprise, I'm able to visualize the next dice roll. It's not haphazard like the card visions were yesterday. I see two bright red cubes marked clearly with white dots like they appear on the green felt in front of me before each roll. The only dice score I can't predict is the one I roll.

This makes absolutely no sense. There's no way I can be reading dice.

It is undeniable a greater force is at work here. This is the manifestation skill Granny constantly rambles on about. The ability to bring something into the present simply by wish and visualization of ownership.

I wished for a hundred thousand dollars a few days ago. Now, I'm bringing it to fruition. I'm not reading the dice. This is divine intervention.

The stack of chips continues to build in front of me. I have this intense, burning desire to count the chips and find out exactly how much I've won. Still, the line from an old Kenny Rogers tape Grandpa Snow used to play echoes in my mind. *You never count your money when you're sittin' at the table; there'll be time enough for countin' when the rolling's done.*

I added the "rolling's" part.

The feeling of manifestation is challenging to explain. It would be the best day of my life, a day where everything went exactly how I hoped, and then I would have to multiply it by a hundred. That would be close to describing the feeling I'm experiencing at the craps table.

A crowd of spectators builds around our table. Most are alive, but a few eternal thrill-seeking spirits are sprinkled in the mix. They all cheer and applaud with each winning roll. They know they are witnessing something extraordinary.

Alvin and the rest of his dead buddies are whipped into a frenzy. Each has become increasingly opaque and brighter with each winning bet.

It's now difficult to discern the dead from the living except for their uncouth adulations. I can't help but laugh at their antics as my pile of chips grows taller and broader.

"What's going on?" Sonia asks from behind me.

I turn to her and say the first thing which comes to mind. "I'm winning a hundred thousand dollars!"

"What?"

Trent appears. "How much do you have?"

I point to the chips. "A crapload!" I begin to laugh a little too manically at my unintended pun.

Trent raises his eyebrows and gives an awkward grin. As my laughter stops, he recovers and asks, "Do you want me to count for you?"

"Please. Oh, how did you do?"

Sonia is animated as she hollers over the crowd noise. "Trent finished in second place. He got his entry fee back plus three thousand dollars."

The living players might think I'm a loon, but I give Sonia a bear hug that she returns with equal fervor.

We did it. Both of us earned precisely what we needed. This is a rare "team win" moment for me, and I'm overcome with joy.

"We did it, April. We won. We can go home now," Sonia says close enough to my ear that I feel the warmth of her breath.

Yeah, about that "going home" thing.

I'm not sure what's going on with my game. If my insane luck is a case of manifestation, I've no clue how I *really* brought it into existence.

I also know there won't be too many days in my life when I can win a hundred thousand dollars. In fact, this is most likely my first and last chance. I can't walk away from this opportunity while I have a hot hand.

Trent finishes counting my chips.

"What's the verdict?" I ask.

Trent draws in a breath that puffs up his chest and smiles. "Over two grand. Nice haul, April."

An additional two grand to the winnings I already stashed in the safe upstairs will be phenomenal. The extra cash will be enough to cover my food and incidental expenses until it's time to move to Atlanta. The sensible thing for me to do is cash out and drive us home.

I glance from Trent to Sonia; both have an expression of expectation, and I know they're tired and thinking it's time to leave. I'd hate to keep them here longer than they care to stay.

Leaning over the table, I pull my chips toward me and then quickly place two on the number eight for a lay bet.

Trent and Sonia will have to get over it. Winning this money could change everything for me.

The spectators break into another round of applause as the dice come up seven, and I win again.

My hand is so hot, maybe I shouldn't roll when it's my turn. I don't want to melt the dice.

Trent and Sonia flank me in support of my effort. I'm going to play out this streak wherever it may lead. I'll be a hero or a zero.

There are scant few live spectators still surrounding the bumper of the table. As the gaming spirits crowd forward, the live guests step back.

I get it. Being bumped by a ghost will raise gooseflesh on anyone regardless of their level of excitement.

I think I like the motley collection of spirits at my table better anyway. They're feeding off the energy of the live spectators and players. Still, I'm feeding off their over-the-top encouragement no one else hears or sees.

Why shouldn't they be excited? I'm invincible. I feel bad I made fun of Granny's manifestation assertions. I sure am glad her beliefs aren't bull malarkey.

It's easier to visualize a hundred-thousand-dollar check in my hand with each passing moment. I envision receiving it from the cashier and mostly putting it in my bank account. Granny always says visualization brings the item into existence quicker.

Something else that'll be quick is my call to Jan Miller. If Master Lloyd and Johnson want this girl, they'll be waiting a long time. I'm going to take a full year off and contemplate all my opportunities. Hey, I don't have to be in a hurry with the bank account I'm going to have.

Who knows, after I take a few weeks to reflect, I might give old Jan a call and tell her I want to buy a partnership. That'll put a crimp in her tail.

My friends wait patiently, but I can sense they're becoming restless. I've almost doubled my pile of chips from when Trent told me I had two thousand dollars. At this rate, I might finally collect my hundred grand a couple weeks after Christmas. I need to put some speed on these winnings.

I hesitate. I should cash out my mountain of chips and walk away. Trent and Sonia need to get home. So, I pull all my chips off the betting section.

Usually, I wouldn't call myself greedy. But the harder I try to convince myself to step away from the table, the more I feel like it's unfinished business.

"April." The familiar voice pierces through the layers of living patrons and excited spiritual gamers. It flows directly into my brain. I glance up from the table, and Memory stands across from me. A barrette on the left side holds her naturally brunette hair away from her face. She wears only a hint of makeup, and she is dressed in a simple, yellow print cotton dress. Classy yet sweet. I realize how young she was when she died. She has the appearance of a high school student visiting her grandparents for the weekend.

"They found her. They found my mama," Memory says.

Tears pop into my eyes as I ask, "Did you get to see her?"

"I did. Mama knows now."

"April." Trent's voice breaks my connection with Memory. "It's your roll."

I take the dice from the stick man and make eye contact with Memory. I mouth "sorry" to her. I wish we could visit, but I have business to attend to.

Memory leans forward and points at the double six. I've been eyeing the bet all night. If this manifestation thing is real, I'd only be helping it along.

What the heck? I push all my chips onto the double six. I came in with nothing.

"What are you doing? That's thirty-four hundred dollars," Trent says as his voice rises an octave.

I do the thirty-to-one math in my head. That is precisely what I'm hoping for, plus a little bit of traveling money. Perfect.

Memory and I share a gaze. She mouths "thank you," and I mouth "you're welcome." I kiss the dice and throw them.

One die pops against the sidewall and lands perfectly still on six. The second die takes a crazy deflection, leaving it spinning on its corner. As it loses steam, the die balances on its side.

Memory leans forward over the edge of the table. She puffs her cheeks and blows as if she is making a birthday wish with candles.

Then she's gone. No trace of her remains. It is so sudden her departure leaves me full of grief.

Chapter 19

The crowd around our craps table erupts into pandemonium. Sonia clutches me at the shoulders as she pogos up and down. I glance at the red dice on the green felt at the end of the table, and my heart stops. Double sixes.

I've won a hundred thousand!

A loud cracking noise reverberates through the casino. A chandelier the size of a large sedan crashes to the floor, casting us into shadows.

I swivel toward the sound. Others break into a run, screaming as they leave. Trent grabs Sonia and me by the arm, pulling us forward.

"Come on," he commands.

"What's going on?" I scream.

He barely looks at me as he pulls us. "Gunshots. It must be a robbery."

Robbery? Who's stupid enough to rob a casino in the middle of the day?

We are caught up in the crush of people vying to escape through one of the two fire escapes at the back of the casino.

Shots ring out again. I peek over my shoulder, and a security guard goes down. A man wearing a black ski mask fires another burst from his automatic rifle at the downed officer.

A second masked man is at the cashiers. His shotgun is trained on the pleasant lady who cut my check yesterday.

She's shoving cash into a gray sports bag. Her eyes bug open, and her cheeks turn radish red.

We've got to get out of here.

I turn my attention back to Trent, who continues to lead us toward a door. There are at least ten people in front of us, and the door is not opening. From the cursing I hear, it may be locked.

The stick man from our craps table is next to me, and he abruptly grunts before falling to the ground. I see a red bloom at the back of his shirt.

"Come on," Trent hollers as he pulls us out of line. "We'll try the other door."

As I let Trent lead us, I look back at the cashiers. The thief with the sports bag is motioning for his partner to follow him out of the casino.

My hope that the attack may be nearing its end is dashed as Rifleman waves off his Bagman. Turning, he aims his assault rifle at the crowd and fires single rounds at a fast clip.

I nearly fall as Trent pulls us through the crowd. I'm bumping into and stepping on people as we go.

Bagman hollers one more time for Rifleman to follow him, appears to give up, and sprints for the front door.

Two more people directly in front of us fall in anguish, and I realize those rounds would have struck us if we were a second faster. I'm dazed as I stare down at the wounded guests and am torn between stopping to administer aid or continuing to run to save my own life.

"Run, and don't you dare look back!" Trent shouts as he leaves us in the chaotic crowd. I watch in horror as he runs toward Rifleman. On the way, he grabs a craps stick and holds it like a spear—with a severely bent tip—as he charges.

Everything plays out in slow motion.

Rifleman is looking to his right, aiming at the cashier who takes cover behind a slot machine. Rifleman's white teeth gleam from the hole in his black mask.

Trent, in a full-out sprint, nears Rifleman. My body tenses in anticipation of Trent cold-cocking the evil man upside his head with the stick.

At the last second, Rifleman notices Trent approaching and swings his gun. Blood mist sprays off Trent's back, and the craps stick splinters into the air.

Sonia and I scream as Trent falls to the floor face first. His body slides a few inches after impacting the carpet.

Rifleman, in turn, goes to one knee. Blood seeps between his fingers as he clutches his hand to his neck. His gun rests against his body, hooked to a sling.

I feel Sonia leave my side, and like a fool, I follow her as we rush toward Trent, lying motionless on the carpet.

Sonia comes to a stop in front of Rifleman. She raises her leg upward in a high kick worthy of a Friday night halftime performance during state playoffs. Her foot connects square on his chin, propelling him upward before landing on his back.

I jump and land with my knees on Rifelman's chest. From muscle memory training with my brothers, I quickly remove the clip from the AR-15 and clear the chambered round.

Rifleman is out cold. I'm not even sure he is still breathing.

The struggle to pull oxygen into my lungs is real. I can't get my breathing under control, much less my nerves.

A shrill, loud scream pierces my brain, causing me to duck involuntarily. I can't tell if it's real or some random noise in my head reverberating through the casino.

I turn toward the noise. Sonia drapes herself over Trent as she lets out another scream accompanied by a wet sob.

Bear crawling over to the two of them, I push her back. She fights me momentarily.

There is blood everywhere.

"If you don't want to lose him, we have to slow the bleeding!" I scream at her.

Sonia continues to resist me. I can tell by the crazed expression in her eyes she is unaware of her actions. I must get through to her.

"Do you want to save him or not?"

Her eyebrows draw together as she whimpers, "Yes."

"Help me get Trent on his side. I need to see an exit wound."

Sonia helps me, and I confirm Trent was hit with a single round that passed clear through. Unfortunately, that's where the good news ends. The bullet went just to the left of his heart and above the lung.

Closing my eyes, I try unsuccessfully to force the words from my mind. My brothers' voices ring in my mind, "a center mass kill shot."

No. This can't happen.

I place my hands on both sides of Trent. "Sonia, place your hands on mine and push as hard as possible. We have to slow his bleeding until the paramedics get here."

Her eyes bug open, but dutifully she does as I request.

As I exert as much pressure as I can on the wound, I feel the blood flow warm and thick in between my fingers. I'm not sure if this will work, but it's the only thing I can think of until help arrives.

Other security guards flood the floor, and two of them handcuff Rifleman. He never moves a muscle. He is losing as much blood as Trent due to the gory injury to his neck.

The palms of my hands itch and burn against Trent's wound. I nearly jerk my hands back in response to the foreign sensation. But I can't. I can't remove the pressure needed to slow his bleeding.

Besides, I have an idea of what might be happening. It wigs me out that my speculation might be correct, but if I can help my friend, I'll just have to deal.

Nana, my mama's mom, used to tell us stories about her grandmother, who was able to heal cuts by laying her hands on the injury. It's just part of the shtick Nana does whenever she talks about the Native American ancestry on her side of the family.

I don't give credence to any of her medicine woman fantasies. I refuse to believe my hands are burning. They are tingling because they have fallen asleep.

Trent's blood stops pouring through my fingers because of the tremendous pressure Sonia and I exert on his wound. At least that's my explanation to myself, and I'm sticking with it.

"Where are the paramedics?" I yell over my shoulder.

Sonia is sobbing uncontrollably. Snot streams track down to the top of her lip. Her mascara runs in dark rivulets down her cheeks, but she holds her small hands firmly against mine.

"Hey, look at me."

She tilts her head up. Her lips tremble. "What?"

"He'll be fine. You know he is tough. Heck, you're both fighters."

"But he was shot." She sobs. "There is too much blood."

"I know. It's a lot, and it is scary. But he'll be fine."

"How do you know?" She tries to wipe her nose on her shoulder and misses.

"I just do. This will only be a cool scar on Trent in a few months. You dig scars, don't you? C'mon, my brothers have always claimed us chicks dig scars. "

Sonia chokes out a laugh. "You ain't right, April."

She doesn't know the half of it. "I get that a lot."

Two paramedics rush toward us and kneel at our side. Each unwraps a wound compress.

With the compress in one hand, they remove our hands from Trent's injury with their other. They apply the field dress coagulant bandages and strap Trent to a stretcher.

Sonia doesn't say a word to me as she follows the stretcher out of the pit. She has one hand clamped onto Trent's foot and never looks back.

They disappear into the hallway, and I exhale a breath I think I've been holding for hours. The floodgates open, and tears rain from my eyes to the carpet. I roll back onto my butt from my kneeling position and pull my knees into my chest. The tears turn to sobs, and I bury my face against my thighs.

Fudge! What just happened?

I saw a man shot in the back, a foot over from me, and I'd be the one with a hole in my back lying on the floor if not for a few inches.

What would've happened to everyone trapped in the casino if Trent hadn't fought back?

Who attacks an armed gunman with a stick?

A fighter. A fighter with something to lose.

Trent better recover. I believe I stopped the bleeding. The question unanswered is if I was in time to save him.

Something warm brushes against my wrist. I look up as Leon squats next to me with a wet towel from the snack bar. Beads of sweat are prominent on his bald head, and his color is pasty.

"For your hands. To wash the blood off."

"Thanks," I say as I take the towel and wipe my hands clean.

Leon surveys the room as the last of the first responders leaves. "Is your friend going to be all right?"

"I hope so."

On a deep sigh, he says, "What idiots. What were they thinking?"

"Stupid people make stupid plans." I start to get up, and he extends his hand.

"You want a cup of coffee?"

A derisive laugh escapes me. "I don't think I need any more adrenaline boosters today."

Chapter 20

Waiting in our room for a call from Sonia, I'm so nervous I have gnawed all my fingernails to the quick. It's a good thing I'm not as limber as I was in high school, or my pedicure would be in danger.

The knock on the door causes me to nearly jump out of my skin. *It must be news about Trent. Please let it be good.*

"Hello? Who is it?" I ask with my hand on the deadbolt.

"Hotel management, may I have a word with you?"

That's odd that the call from the hospital would have come to the hotel rather than me. "One second."

I open the door. A very contrite-looking man with a dark bronze complexion framed by white hair stares dolefully at me. "Ms. Jurgenson, I apologize for the intrusion. I'm Dick Guidry, the hotel manager."

"Oh, no. I'm not Sonia."

His dark eyes narrow, and he glances at the number on the door. "I apologize. I was attempting to get in contact with the woman traveling with Trent Orr."

I place my hand on my chest. "I'm one of the women traveling with him—them—I'm their friend."

His mouth opens as his chin rises. "Oh, my. I'm terribly sorry. You're Ms. Snow. The woman who has the claim from the craps table."

"I wouldn't exactly call it a claim. I did win." I don't feel like arguing the point, given things could have ended much worse for me."

His lips tighten as he nods his head. "Yes. I understand. It's a regrettable situation. With Russell being gunned down and the rest of the guests dispersed, I'm afraid there is nobody to corroborate your winnings."

I suppose Russell was the name of my dealer. The vision of him going down next to me as we ran for the exit flashes in my mind. I don't know what my expression is, but it makes Dick shift his weight.

"Normally, we would simply review the security tape as we have multiple cameras on every game table." His brow furrows. "Unfortunately, the tapes all have some sort of magnetic disruption on them?"

I squint and tilt my head.

He frowns uncomfortably. "The bottom three-fourths of the tapes were just TV snow."

"Tapes?" I ask.

He clears his throat. "Yes. All four recordings.

I contain my laugh, but my chest bounces up and down. Of course. Why would I believe anything different?

"So, you're going to keep the hundred thousand dollars I won because your security failed to keep us safe, and your security equipment is faulty. Is that what I'm hearing?"

Dick widens his stance. "I assure you that we will make good immediately if we recover anything that confirms your winnings. It is a requirement of the gaming commission. Even if it weren't, our reputation as a fair establishment is important to our longevity."

My argument isn't with Dick Guidry. It's with the two idiots that thought it would be a great idea to rob a casino and, in the process, shot my friend.

"I'm sorry. I'm just on edge since I have not received word about my friend's condition yet," I say.

"No. Please don't apologize, Ms. Snow. This has been a difficult day for all of us. One we will never be able to forget. A very tragic day indeed."

I stare at the floor as the events of the attack play through my mind again. "Yes. I never will forget today."

"I know it is an incredibly small show of gratitude, but I want you to know that the hotel will be covering your friend's medical bill and the expense of the room. His heroic actions allowed the rest of the security team to react, and he saved many more patrons from harm."

Thinking of Trent bleeding out on the floor, my throat tightens, and I can't say anything. I nod my head in appreciation.

"Is there anything else I can do for you at this time, Ms. Snow?"

I open my mouth to say no when I have an epiphany. "Mr. Guidry, did you work here in the nineties."

"I'm the original manager. I've been in charge since the day the hotel opened."

"Does the name Brodie mean anything to you?"

Dick flinches. "No, I can't say that it does."

"A security guard in the nineties. About six feet tall, two hundred pounds, sort of serious, and looked good in a suit. You had to have known him."

Dick swallows loudly. "Oh, Brodie—Brodie Chauvin. Yes. Of course, I remember him."

"You wouldn't know where I might find him, would you?"

Dick's façade crumbles, "Is this some a sick joke because of what happened to Jolly today? If so, know that I do not find it the slightest bit amusing."

Who the heck is Jolly? I lean into the conversation. "Partly, but it's imperative that I get in contact with him immediately."

"Who are you with?"

"Pardon?"

Dick gestures with his hands. "What news agency are you with? Just because they found that girl the same day he has a stroke doesn't mean anything."

What the devil is he talking about? "Brodie?"

"No! Now, what news agency."

"I'm not with the news, but if you put me in touch with Brodie

Chauvin, I can help clear up the Memory Reid case."

Dick points his finger at me. "Memory Reid? If you are not a reporter, why are you bringing that girl's name up."

"What is the problem here? I'm trying to help. Just tell me where to find Brodie, and once I talk to him, it will clear everything up."

"You know darn well you can't talk to Brodie."

"I only need to talk to him."

"Then you better be a psychic!"

This is my turn to flinch. We stare at one another until I'm sure he does not know that I am a psychic.

"Brodie hung himself in the staff showers twenty years ago. His partner found him. A note was found in his locker the next day when we cleared it out." Dick sighs. "I can't get Memory out of my memory. God forgive me."

A chill runs up my spine. Brodie killed himself? So, he had remorse for the accident and for hiding her body. It doesn't absolve him, but it makes him more human than a monster—partially.

Dick smirks. "But you already know that don't you, Ms. Snow —if that is your real name? Just like you know that Jolly Landry had a massive stroke while getting a CT scan for cancer right after learning that Memory's body had been found."

Jolly—Jolly Landry—why does that name sound so familiar? I touch the wall to steady myself as the room spins.

"Ms. Snow?" Dick's expression changes to concern. "You don't look well."

I wave him off. "I'm alright."

"I'm sorry. I shouldn't have said those things. It's been a terribly stressful day."

"No. I understand. And I'm not a reporter, but I thank you for telling me about Brodie."

He bites his lower lip. "Yes. I shouldn't have said anything about that, either. Other than his wife and a few employees, nobody knows."

I gesture him toward the door. "I assure you, nobody will ever hear about it from me."

"I appreciate your discretion, Ms. Snow."

The door closes, and I lean against the cool, metal surface. As I consider the new information, my hand steals into my pocket, and I toy with the round hoop.

As I pull it out and examine the tarnished hoop, the name Jolly continues to echo in my head. I sit down on the bed and listen to the voice. It is so much further away than normal spirit voices. It is as if it is an echo from another day years ago.

My body jolts, and I am looking at the floorboard of a car. "Jolly! I think she's waking up."

"Calm down, Brodie. It's just the motion from the car."

My head is killing me.

"Jolly, I swear her eyes opened."

"Dude, that's normal. Just close her lids again—and make sure not to let her bleed on my seat. You're keeping her head on that towel I gave you. Right?"

"Yes, Jolly." Brodie rubs his hands over my eyes, and I hold my lids shut while I consider my situation.

"I swear you screwed the pooch this time, Brodie. I can't believe you allowed that little girl to get us into this pickle."

"It wasn't my fault, Jolly. She jerked away from me, and the next thing I know, she fell off the curb and her head began to bleed out."

"It wasn't my fault, Jolly," the driver mocks.

I try to move, but my arms and legs won't respond correctly.

The car comes to a stop.

"Get out and open the gate, Brodie."

The rear door at my feet opens and closes. The car rolls forward.

It's okay. I know what happens this time. If I can get my legs to work, I should be able to push the sarcophagus lid off once these two men leave.

The door at my head opens. "Her eyes are open again, Jolly!"

"I swear, Brodie. Quit being such an idiot. It's because of the motion of the car. Now get her out, and let's get the lid off this grave."

My arms are pulled over my head, and I am pulled out of the car.

It feels like I break a couple of ribs as I land on a rock.

I'm drug a little further. Hands slide under my midsection and flip me over.

"I hate this happened," Brodie whines.

"How about you cry in your beer about it later. Help me slide this cover. Make sure not to go too far."

I hear voices, and I look to my left periphery. The oak tree faces are grinning and licking their lips.

"Jolly, her eyes!"

"Brodie, how many times do I have to tell you—she blinked!"

"That's what I was trying to say."

"Blast it. You can't even screw up all the way. Everything is half done with you. Pick up that rock and finish her off."

"What?"

"I said pick up that rock and finish what you started."

"Jolly, she's alive. Let's take her to the hospital."

"We can't take her to the hospital, you fool. Do I always have to do everything for you?"

A face comes into view. Above his head, he holds a huge rock. My breathing halts as I recognize a younger Pit Boss.

Jolly is the pit boss I diagnosed this morning.

"Turn her over, Brodie. She is staring at me."

I feel hands slide under my midsection again and flip me over. Before my body stops rocking, my vision stops.

Chapter 21

I continue to rub the hoop earring in between my fingers. The vision has ended, the gold is warm from my touch, and my heart is broken.

There are times I wish my curiosity did not drive me so hard. The brutality I often find with answers is more than I can bear.

I call Sonia's phone again. This time she picks up. I hope for the best and brace for the worst.

"How is he?"

"He's out of surgery and resting now," she whispers.

"I'm so relieved, Sonia. I was worried."

"Me too." Her voice cracks.

"I was going to come up and keep you company. Can I bring you something?"

"No. Please don't bother. There's only this beat-up chair in his room. It wouldn't be large enough for both of us."

I feel awkward. You can't force comfort on somebody when they insist on pushing you away. But I've seen the same behavior from my parents on a few occasions. "Sure. I understand. Promise me if you change your mind, you'll call me."

"I will. We'll meet up in the morning. I'm sorry, I know you're probably ready to get back home."

"No worries. Try to get some rest, and I'll see you in the morning."

I'm hanging up, and she says, "Hey, April. I want to tell you—well—I'm not sure what you did, but thank you."

My ears heat as extra blood rushes to them. "What do you mean, Sonia?"

"Trent's bleeding. I thought he was dead. I thought it was pointless when you told me to hold my hands to yours, but somehow, he stopped bleeding. It's a miracle."

What do I say to not sound like a freak? "We got lucky, Sonia. Some days it's the best you can hope for."

I push the last of Trent's clothes into his duffel and start on Sonia's makeup case. I admit I'm feeling slightly down despite the fact we escaped death and earned the money we only dreamed we could win on our crazy spur-of-the-moment trip.

I secure their cash winnings from the first day in my purse. To me, the envelope symbolizes their hopes and dreams. Their future with plans built on a foundation as shaky as a house of cards weighs heavy on my mind.

Darn it. Somewhere along the way, those two wild kids worked their way into my heart.

Mostly I think I'm feeling lonely again. And yes, I'm a little sorry for myself and, if I'm honest, a tinge envious. Will, I ever experience the "all in" type of love? I mean, I'm not looking for a man who will charge a possessed man firing an assault rifle. But somebody who would stand up for me even when it's uncomfortable? Is it too much for a girl to wish? If he's out there, he's invisible.

My options are to binge on every dessert in the casino since I have an open meal ticket. Or I can curl into a ball on Sonia and Trent's bed while I count the ways my life sucks.

My cell phone rings. It sort of interrupts my pity party. I'm surprised to see it's my cousin Tricia from Nashville.

She fills me in on her dad's recent retirement. They have leased a house in Pensacola for a month as a celebration, and she invites me to come down.

I like the beach. Things are looking up for April.

Visiting hours have just begun as I make it to the hospital the following day. I'm eager to get on the road to Pensacola and start my visit with Tricia. I also need to go by the bank to wire my rent money to the apartment manager.

When I open the door to Trent's room, the number of tubes running out of him catches me by surprise. I don't know what I expect. The man was shot through the chest.

I set their luggage just inside the room, and Sonia ushers me in. She sits on the edge of his bed, and I sit on the recliner. "Is he still doing well?"

There are dark bags under Sonia's eyes. "Yes. They think he's going to make a full recovery."

"I'm so happy, Sonia."

We fall into an awkward silence. That is my cue. I reach into my purse and smile as I pull out their winnings envelope. "Your winnings from the first day."

"Thanks. I totally forgot about the money in the safe."

"The winnings from the tourney?"

Sonia rubs her face. "In my purse."

"Good."

"I suppose. I wish now we listened to you and left the night before."

"No. Don't even think about making this your fault. The evil jerk caused this, not you two deciding to stay another day and play. It was all his doing."

"I know. But I still wonder what if we had left."

We sit in silence and listen to Trent's steady breathing. The longer I stare at everything he's hooked up to, the more surreal yesterday's events are to me.

"I forgot to ask you if they paid you your winnings."

It wasn't funny, but I couldn't help but smile. "Well, all the security cameras pointed at our table were mostly recording a blur. Sort of like when a VHS tape dies."

"So, what? They're not gonna pay because they say their cameras weren't working?"

The cameras were working, but the excess energy field caused by the crush of supernatural spectators gathered around the table to cheer me on, creating a reflective barrier. The energy field played havoc with the cameras' ability to record the table surface. But I don't want to explain how I know, so I omit that part of the story. "Hey, I know I won, and the biggest win of the day is the three of us survived to play another day."

"Well, I'm not gonna say you're not right, but you're definitely taking it a lot better than I'd be able to."

"But speaking of money, you two won everything you said you needed. The next time I'm up in Marshall County watching the local news, I expect to see there's a children's art center opening up with you as the director."

The stress and fatigue of the last twenty-four hours miraculously disappear from Sonia, and she glows. "You know it."

I guess I do. Sonia and Trent are a couple I would never bet against.

I pull in for a Coke and candy bar at a gas station on the way out of town. Since I feel like my hundred-thousand-dollar manifestation is still in play, I spend five dollars on a 'Hundred K' scratch-off card.

I set my card on the counter before me, focusing all my energy on winning the grand prize. Full of expectation, I scratch the silver gum from the card.

I push. The card says I get another card free.

Granny—what a corker. I can't believe I got sucked into her nonsense.

I go back to the cashier to turn in my card for another try. A young mom in front of me tells her daughter to put a candy bar back. The little girl appears devastated but minds her mother.

I don't think it's fair to the mom or the little girl for retail stores to position the candy at children's eye level. I pull a five out of my purse.

"Do you mind if I treat?" I ask the mom.

She starts to say no. The mom reconsiders as she searches my face and smiles. "Jody, what do you tell the nice lady?"

The little girl glances up at me. "Thank you, nice lady."

"You're welcome, cutie."

Something opens in my aching heart, and I take a long breath. The little girl stares with quizzical eyes, and her lips turn into a smile.

All the stress and pressure of the last few days leaves my body in a rush, replaced with an uplifting thought. There is always hope in this world. Sometimes we only need to be in the presence of someone who has not yet been jaded. I place the game card on top of the five-dollar bill and hand it to the mom.

"And this is for you."

Her eyebrows draw together in confusion as she examines the card.

"You're going to win the hundred grand," I say over my shoulder as I leave the store.

As I turn my car toward Pensacola, I know I'm the luckiest girl in the world.

The End

April May Snow's story continues with

Throw the Elbow

Don't miss the next April May Snow release date. Join the reader's club now.

www.mscottswanson.com

M. Scott lives near Nashville, Tennessee, with his wife and two guard chihuahuas. When he is not writing, he cooks or takes long walks to smooth out plotlines for the next April May Snow adventure.

Dear Reader,

Thank you for reading April's story. You make her adventures possible. Without you, there would be no point in creating her story.

I'd like to encourage you to post a review on Amazon. A favorable critique from you is a powerful way to support authors you enjoy. It allows our books to be found by additional readers, and frankly, motivates us to continue to produce books. This is especially true for your independents.

Once again, thank you for the support. You are the magic that breathes life into these characters.

M. Scott Swanson

The best way to stay in touch is to join the reader's club!

www.mscottswanson.com

Other ways to stay in touch are:

Like on Amazon

Like on Facebook

Like on Goodreads

You can also reach me at mscottswanson@gmail.com.

I hope your life is filled with

magic and LOVE!

Made in the USA
Monee, IL
31 January 2023

25835324R00080